THE
WOLF

D0839641

THE NERO WOLFE FILES

EDITED BY MARVIN KAYE

WILDSIDE PRESS

THE NERO WOLFE FILES

For more information, contact:
Wildside Press, www.wildsidepress.com

ACKNOWLEDGMENTS

THANKS TO the officers and Steering Committee of The Wolfe Pack for permission to select and republish contents of *The Gazette,* contents of which are property of the Pack.

Thanks to all its editors over the years, in chronological order: Lawrence F. Brooks and Patricia Dreyfus, John McAleer (Consulting Editor), Ellen Krieger, Ettagale Blauer, Susan E. Dahlinger, Bill DeAndrea, Sarah Montague, Alexandra Franklin, J. G. O'Boyle, Henry W. Enberg II, Beverly Norris, Joel Levy, Sandy Olubas (Associate Editor), Joe Sweeney, Carol Novak (Web Master), and Jean Quinn. The City Editor, of course, has always been Lon Cohen.

I am deeply thankful for the aid and support of Barbara and Rebecca Stout, the late John McAleer and his son Andrew, and owner of New York City's splendid *The Mysterious Bookshop* Otto Penzler.

Inestimable thanks to Steering Committee member Kevin Gordon for allowing us to use his splendid portrait of Mr. Wolfe for the cover of this book.

Anyone wishing to purchase prints of them should get in touch with The Wolfe Pack via its web site: http://www.nerowolfe.org

Thanks to the following Wolfe Pack members for contributing titles to this anthology — William Kost, for *The Nero Wolfe Files;* Ettagale Blauer for *Stoutly Wolfe;* Tenby Storm for *Wolfe Tracks,* and Dr. B. T. See, of Singapore, for *Nero Wolfe Redux.*

Special thanks to Wolfe Pack Treasurer Saralee Kaye for support and assistance, and love and thanks to my college roommate and pal Dave Ossar for first introducing me to (actually, *insisting* that I read) Nero Wolfe, and to the late W. S. Baring-Gould for his book, *Nero Wolfe of West 35th Street*.

CONTENTS

Appendices

INTRODUCTION

I FIRST met Nero Wolfe while I was an undergraduate theatre student at Penn State.

Now I've never been much of a mystery reader, preferring fantasy and science fiction, but there are some exceptions: Sherlock Holmes, of course, Dashiell Hammett (but not Raymond Chandler), anything by Dick Francis, Anthony Berkeley's richly comic, brilliantly plotted *Trial and Error*, Leo Perutz's unparalleled *The Master of the Day of Judgment*, and especially the pseudonymous Carter Dickson's locked room and impossible crime murder mysteries starring the outrageously funny, elephantine Sir Henry Merrivale (aka H. M.). John Dickson Carr, author of the H. M. series, said that he modeled his detective on Winston Churchill (though I always pictured him as a dead ringer for that splendid British film actor Francis L. Sullivan). While the intricate plotting in the twenty-plus H. M. novels and two short stories undoubtedly held my interest, it was the comedy that kept me reading. H. M. was always hilarious, especially when he tried to act dignified, not that he was often guilty of that. The laughter became broader as the series continued until in the final novel, *The Cavalier's Cup*, the mystery was seriously upstaged by such antics as H. M.'s upcoming singing debut, much to the horror of everyone within earshot. I never much cared for Carr's other mystery series about Dr. Gideon Fell; the plotting was equally amazing, but Fell just wasn't fun.

Another detective I enjoyed was Dashiell Hammett's "Fat Man," whose adventures I mostly listened to on radio, although I did see (and now own) the movie based on his adventures, and was pleased to see that the actor with the apt name of J. Scott Smart who played the role really was as fat as he sounded when he wheezed his dialogue "on mike."

The film also humorously and quickly establishes the sleuth's consuming interest (pun fully intended) in good food.

So it appears that I have a predisposition for liking oversized ratiocinators. Possibly because my father was fat, and/or possibly because they remind me of one of the funniest fellows who ever graced the silver screen, Mr. Oliver Norvell Hardy.

It was another oversized individual, my college roommate Dave Ossar, who urged me to try reading Rex Stout. I was reluctant at first, not because of my aforementioned lukewarm interest in mysteries, but because of the kind of obsessive behavior one finds in its purest form in book collectors. If it's a series, I want to read it from book one onward, but there are so many Nero Wolfe novels, I just didn't know where to begin.

I can't recall how much urging it took for me to give them a try, out of sequence, nor am I sure which one I read first; I think it was either *Plot It Yourself* or *If Death Ever Slept*. But I do remember I was immediately amused by the narrative tone and the risible idiosyncracies of Mr. Wolfe. Archie annoyed me a bit at first, he was such a wiseass, but that impression didn't last long. Soon I saw he was much more than just another Sam Spade-ish tough guy, and I couldn't help but sympathize with and admire anyone who could deal with the circumscribed order of life in that brownstone on West 35th Street.

I became hooked on Wolfe and Archie, acquired all their adventures, and read them in the order they were written. Eventually I wrote seven mystery novels myself before switching to fantasy and science fiction. My five Hilary Quayle novels, currently published by Wildside Press, deliberately echo the Archie Goodwin style, and their narrator/scribe Gene is supposed to be Archie's cousin, though they're not fond of each other — Archie once confessed he doesn't like the name Eugene. As for Hilary, she is Wolfe's illegitimate daughter.

Another influence during college that led me to begin reading about Nero Wolfe was W. S. Baring-Gould's "official" biography, *Sherlock Holmes of Baker Street*, which proposed the controversial theory that Wolfe is the offspring of Holmes and Irene Adler, from the short story, *A Scandal in Bohemia*. (Baring-Gould later also wrote *Nero Wolfe of 35th Street*.)

After I moved to Manhattan — this is quite some time back, at least twenty years ago — I saw an ad in *The New York Times* which led me to write in and receive a certificate vouching for membership in the West 35th Street Irregulars, signed one L. T. Cramer. I wished such an organization actually existed. Apparently, other folk thought the same, and the list of those who responded to the *Times* found its way into determined hands. A Nero Wolfe-loving organization was formed, scheduled a dinner at the old Gramercy Park Hotel, and lo! an invitation arrived in the mail to attend and partake. My erstwhile wife Saralee and I did so, became charter members and are still members of the Steering Committee; she is the treasurer of The Wolfe Pack.

I've belonged to a number of groups in the past; for many years I was an officer of the Laurel and Hardy society, the Sons of the Desert, but the only organization I've stayed in is The Wolfe Pack because it's more fun than any other I've belonged to, even the Sons.

Beginning with hard work from Ellen Krieger, who was its first president aka werowance, Marjorie Mortensen, Larry Brooks, Professor John McAleer, who wrote the authorized biography of Rex Stout, and others, the Pack recently celebrated its 25th anniversary.

It should be noted that quite a few devotees of Nero Wolfe, such as the late Henry Enberg, show equal enthusiasm about Sherlock Holmes. But quite some time ago in The Wolfe Pack it was determined that the Canon, a term employed by Holmesians to denote the Watsonian chronicles, should not be applied to Archie Goodwin's Nero Wolfe stories. Considering Mr. Wolfe's amplitude, *le mot juste* was determined to be the *Corpus*, and that it is the term you will find employed in *The Nero Wolfe Files*.

The Wolfe Pack holds a Black Orchid Banquet in early December with food chiefly derived from *The Nero Wolfe Cookbook*, which, though officially credited to Rex Stout, was mainly the work of Barbara Burn, Rex's last editor at Viking Press. On the afternoon of the banquet, the annual Assembly is held, consisting of speeches and panel discussions on topics Neronian and Stoutean.

One of the earliest things The Pack did was to establish an annual Nero award for the best American mystery novel of the past year. The award is bestowed at the Black Orchid Banquet. Other events sponsored by the Pack have included Shad Roe Dinners; discussions of all the Nero Wolfe stories, one by one; picnics at High Meadow, the estate where Rex Stout lived and worked; a trip to Canada to visit the cast and crew of the late A&E *Nero Wolfe* TV series; and Brunch Hunts in which teams of Neronians collectively try to figure out clues in order to find the restaurant.

The founding "raceme" of The Wolfe Pack is in New York City, but there are branches in other cities, as well. More about its history and activities are in the second part of this anthology. For further information, including how to join, see the organization's website — http://www.nerowolfe.org — or if you are not a computer person, write to The Wolfe Pack, P.O. Box 230822 Ansonia Station, NYC 10023.

FOR TWENTY-FIVE years The Wolfe Pack has published a more-or-less quarterly magazine called *The Gazette* (what else?). Its pages abound with Neronian articles, verse, fictional pastiches and parodies, quizzes and puzzles, and reports on Pack events, as well as Wolfe Whistles: Nero Wolfe and Rex Stout in the news. A fair number of its articles began as speeches at the Assembly; some were reprints from other sources, notably John McAleer's *Rex Stout Journal*.

The Nero Wolfe Files is a generous sampling of some of the best articles and stories from the pages of *The Gazette*. The operant word in the preceding sentence is *"some."* I regret the abundance of excellent material that did not make the final "cut," and I can only hope that this anthology is sufficiently popular to motivate The Wolfe Pack to want a second such collection in the not-too-distant future. Meanwhile, thanks to the efforts involved in putting *The Nero Wolfe Files* together, the late John McAleer's son Andrew has agreed to a Wildside Press reissue in one volume of his father's extended interviews of Rex Stout and his sister.

The Nero Wolfe Files differs from every other anthology I have edited over the years in two significant ways. First, it was not possible to write rubrics to each individual selection. I regret this; much of my genre literature education came from reading the head-notes in *Ellery Queen's Mystery Magazine* and *The Magazine of Fantasy and Science Fiction*. Unfortunately, many authors in this book were inaccessible and I could not ask them for personal data. Rather than single out the comparatively few I know or knew, I opted for brief subsection lead-ins. The second difference in *The Nero Wolfe Files* is that it breaks my rule that no author should appear more than once in a single anthology. The nature of The Wolfe Pack is such that some of the best pieces contributed to *The Gazette* were written by devoted members whom the editors could rely upon for ongoing contributions to issue after issue.

A FEW DETAILS concerning editing — Book page references have mostly been eliminated since which edition referred to seldom was specified by the authors. Editorial notes by *Gazette* editors, when included, appear in brackets prefaced by ED., whereas my notes and explications end with — MK.

When names of individual Nero Wolfe cases appear in *The Gazette*, they are usually designated by abbreviations, a complete list of which always appears on the inside back cover of each issue. Novels are in capital letters, I. e. RANG means *The Doorbell Rang*, while short stories are lower case, e. g., diel which stands for "*Die Like a Dog.*" I opted to write them out and set them in italics, with the titles of short stories embraced by quotation marks.

Finally, there is the question of spoilers, such as the naming of the murderer in a particular book or story. If it was a matter of a word or two, or a brief phrase, I have deleted it. But some articles would have been hamstrung by such editing, so when that is the case, a warning note will enable the reader to avoid that selection for the time being.

Now it's time to uncap the beer, pour it carefully and adjust the bead (I had to look that term up to see that it wasn't a misprint for "head") and settle back into the red leather chair. If we're in luck, Wolfe will be in a gracious mood . . . and if we're very fortunate, he'll ask us that all-important question, "Have you eaten?!"

Marvin Kaye
66 West 35th Street, NY
September 2004

REX TREMENDAE

IT IS fitting that this portion of *The Nero Wolfe Files* should begin and end with the name McAleer. John, the father, pursued his scholarly appreciation and personal enthusiasm for Nero Wolfe to its logical extreme by becoming a friend of the author and his family and receiving their permission to write *Rex Stout: A Biography* (Little, Brown, 1977). Andrew, his son, is an attorney whose interest and knowledge in his father's Stoutean endeavours makes his an invaluable link in the ongoing devotion of The Wolfe Pack to the *Corpus* and the genius (literally) who created it.

Professor McAleer's superb overview of the series and the author, "Nero Wolfe: A Retrospective," appeared in the Autumn 1984 *Gazette* (Volume III # 4), as did the touching memorial to Rex's wife, Pola Weinberg Stout, by Eleanor Sullivan, longtime editor of *Ellery Queen's Mystery Magazine*. The chronology of the series and associated books appeared in the premier issue and was compiled by Stephen F. Schultheis; I have updated it.

A trio of personal reminiscences that provide fascinating insight into Rex Stout's character is featured in this section: "Working with Rex Stout," the transcription of Barbara Benjamin's 2003 speech to The Wolfe Pack in which she told what it was like to be secretary to Archie Goodwin's "agent" (Spring 2003 *Gazette*, Volume XV, #1); "A Meeting of Minds," Marion S. Wilcox's correspondence with Rex Stout as one of his most devoted fans (*The Gazette*, Summer and Autumn 1979, Volume I #s 3 and 4), and Barbara Burn's "Recipe for a Cookbook," from the *Gazette*'s premier issue (Winter 1979). Rex's last editor at Viking Press, Barbara was both the motivating spirit, and essentially the real author of "The Nero Wolfe Cookbook," the "Bible" that The Wolfe Pack consults when planning the menus of its annual banquets.

Charles E. Burns provides an intriguing glimpse of Rex Stout's work during World War II (*The Gazette*, Fall 1998, Volume XII # 4), while Robert Franks speculates with arguable but undeniable skill on the relationship between Rex Stout, Nero Wolfe and Lawrence of Arabia (*The Gazette*, Spring 1998, Volume XII # 3).

Michael Jaffe was executive producer of A&E's *Nero Wolfe* TV series, enthusiastically received by many Wolfe Pack members. His remarks as the main speaker at the 2001 Black Orchid Banquet were transcribed in the Fall 2001 *Gazette*, erroneously designated Volume XVI, though it was actually Volume XIV # 2.

Rex Stout's personal musings, provided by Andrew McAleer, are in the Fall 1998 *Gazette* (Volume XII # 4), and Andrew McAleer is also the source of the Isaac Asimov toast, written impromptu at a Black Orchid Banquet at the prompting of John McAleer.

NERO WOLFE:
A RETROSPECTIVE

by John McAleer

WHEN IN 1934, at the age of ninety-three, U.S. Supreme Court Justice Oliver Wendell Holmes read Rex Stout's *Fer-de-Lance*, he wrote on the margin of the last page, "This fellow is the best of them all." Holmes did not live to see his judgment vindicated over and over again, but others who shared his enthusiasm at the time survived to confirm his astuteness. Forty years later, when Rex Stout, at eighty-nine, published his seventy-second and final Nero Wolfe story, *A Family Affair* (1975), novelist Walter D. Edmonds declared: "I shall never forget my excitement on reading *Fer-de-Lance*, sprung like Athena perfect from the Jovian brow, fresh and new and at the same time with enough plain familiar things in scene and setting to put any reader at his ease. That in my mind is Rex Stout's secret, and with each new Nero Wolfe it has jelled more perfectly."

From its first appearance *Fer-de-Lance* has been recognized as one of the cornerstone works of detective fiction. In fact, the *Times* of London soon put it on its list of the one hundred best detective stories ever written. One of the many remarkable attributes of the novel that justify this verdict is the thoroughness with which it sets in place a framework sturdy and intricate enough to sustain an epic that ultimately would encompass more than ten thousand pages. This framework appears, of course, to depend on a system of comic order that Wolfe has ordained for himself and those living under his roof and which outsiders,

whether clients or intruders — and that includes the constabu-
lary (the FBI as well as New York's Finest) — are compelled to
recognize and accommodate. Wolfe holds to an unvarying reg-
imen. He will not leave his brownstone house on West Thirty-
fifth Street on business. (Perhaps as many as a score of times he
violates this rule, but, over a period of more than forty years, that
amounts to no more than an infinitesimal breach of conduct).
Women are given no role in his meticulously-managed household, yet the housekeeping arrangements are flawless. For that
reason, Clara Fox, in *The Rubber Band* (1936), is moved to say,
"'You know, Mr. Goodwin, this house represents the most inso-
lent denial of female rights the mind of man has ever conceived.
No woman in it from top to bottom, but the routine is faultless,
the food is perfect, and the sweeping and dusting impeccable.'"

Wolfe eats breakfast in his bedroom at eight. Between nine
and eleven he tends his ten thousand orchid plants in his rooftop
greenhouse. From eleven till one-fifteen he is in his office, and
then after lunch he is there until four. From four to six he again
sojourns, virtually incommunicado, among his orchids. He
returns then to his office, where he stays till his dinner hour,
seven-thirty. Only in the most extraordinary circumstances does
he tolerate any breach of this routine. Actually, however, Wolfe
perceives that the order he decrees within his own household is
a working model — a microcosm if you will — of that ideal order
that civilization must move toward if it is to endure and prevail.

That Rex Stout should, from the outset, regulate with
clocklike precision the context of the world in which Nero Wolfe
would function comes as no surprise to those who knew him.
A genius in his own right (he had an IQ of 185), it was usual with
him, at the outset of a new enterprise, to visualize it right down
to its most minute articulations, because he wanted to be certain
it could stand up under every stress and strain before he set it in
motion. This he had done, in 1916, with the school banking
system — the Educational Thrift Service — that earned millions
of dollars for the Stout family in the years before he turned to
writing. For three days he locked himself in his room at the

Schenley Hotel, in Pittsburgh, brainstorming every particular of it before it was launched.

The relentless logic that Nero Wolfe applies to the problems that beset him found its pattern in the flawlessly functioning mind of Rex Stout — a mind that enabled Stout to write his stories with such assurance that he got them right on first try. Sometimes he leaned his head against his typewriter until the frame grew hot, plotting the next step, but when he struck the keys he was certain of what he wanted to say. The first draft was always the final draft. When he pulled the last page from the typewriter, the manuscript was ready to put in the mail. Writing four to six pages a day, in a nine-hour stint, he usually finished a book in thirty-eight days. "If I had to rewrite a book to get it right," Rex said, "I would have done so. But I never had to." Lucetta Stout, Rex's mother, once said that she named him Rex "because when he came out, he came out like a king." Nero Wolfe also came out like a king.

Over many years various explanations have been advanced to account for the favor detective fiction finds with a multitude of readers. Somerset Maugham thought it found its public among those who like their stories well made. Ronald Knox surmised it is popular because man, by nature, is a puzzle-solving animal. Phoebe Atwood Taylor mischievously alleged that it gives men a chance to channel off their hostilities by allowing them to participate vicariously in the act of murder. Edgar Allan Poe suggested that it justified itself by exercising the mind in the pursuit of its proper end — the attainment of truth. Charles Brady proposed that it commends itself to serious notice because it upholds fixed moral values in an increasingly relativistic world. Rex Stout himself whimsically contended that it owes its acceptance to its success in perpetuating the illusion that man is a rational animal. The essence of these many claims is distilled in Mark Van Doren's declaration that "the detective story must remain civilized because that is what the literature of detection is all about; the protection of civilization by those courageous and competent enough to save it." Because Rex Stout realized this fact, Van Doren concluded, he "never subscribed to the theory that the detective must be a thug, a drunkard, and a lecher." Indeed, sex and violence have only a small role to play in the Wolfe Corpus. Yet Rex Stout was no prude. "Sex and violence," he told me, "like all other items of human behavior, are acceptable and desirable in a detective story if they are essential to the story. In mine, apparently, they are not."

In a compelling assessment of the saga of Nero Wolfe, David Anderson sees the cycle of stories steadily broadening from a concern with personal order, as embodied in the individual family, e.g., *The League of Frightened Men* (1935), *The Red Box* (1936), *Too Many Cooks* (1938), *Some Buried Caesar* (1939), and *Where There's a Will* (1941); to a concern with political order, embodied in the state, e.g., *Over My Dead Body* (1939), *The Silent Speaker* (1946), and *The Second Confession* (1949); to a concern with ethical order, which upholds man's place in the scheme of creation, e.g., *The Final Deduction* (1961), *A Right to Die* (1964), and *Death of a Doxy* (1966).

While Nero Wolfe is preeminently a man of intellect — a veritable embodiment of reason — simultaneously, as he readily and frequently acknowledges, he is an ardent romantic, cherishing a vision of an ideal society. Within his brownstone house he can anticipate some success in securing and maintaining the ideal order that he envisages. Yet, as David Anderson observes, "His daily schedule is as much an insistence on order as a tribute to it." To the extent that it is possible for him to do so, he isolates himself to safeguard his romantic vision. He even accounts for his obesity (in peak form he weighs 287 pounds) as a condition fostered to insulate himself from emotions. His alleged misogyny is ascribed to the same cause. As he says in *Too Many Cooks*, "'Not like women? They are astounding and successful animals. For reasons of convenience, I merely preserve an appearance of immunity.'" This does not keep him from instructing Archie, on occasion, to seat an attractive lady client where he can observe a well-turned calf.

But Wolfe has no more chance of limiting his struggle for

order to his own carefully-manipulated environment than Poe's potentate in *"The Masque of the Red Death"* had of isolating his household from the pestilence raging outside the confines of his subterranean palace. Even his right to isolate himself in this fashion may be questioned, just as Doctor Joseph Fletcher, the eminent situation ethics expert, questioned the propriety of isolating David, "the bubble boy," from the hazards of a world nature had not fitted him to cope with. The ideal human community Wolfe seeks to create, the chaotic world beyond his doors — the point of origin of many harsh intrusions — and, ironically, Wolfe's dependency on that chaos for the money he needs to underwrite his fantasy of an ideal world are irreconcilable, and the issues involved must, of course, ultimately be confronted.

As much as Wolfe reverences his ideal environment, he is not blind to reality. In *"Door to Death"* (1950), he tells Joseph G. Pitcairn, "'It would be foolhardy to assume that you would welcome a thorn for the sake of such abstractions as justice or truth, since that would make you a rarity almost unknown.'" Yet Nero Wolfe himself is such a rarity. When he confronts the crime lord, Arnold Zeck, in *In the Best Families* (1950), he realizes that the safety and stability of the brownstone will exist as a mere sham if he does not meet the challenge Zeck has thrown to him. Accordingly, he abandons his snug, secure haven and goes forth into the world to suffer what, for him, are unspeakable indignities before he brings his quarry to ground. It was not with irreverence that Stout caused Wolfe to abandon his sanctuary, leaving the door ajar behind him, on Easter Sunday, for he, too, in secular terms, was coming forth as a savior who had voluntarily assumed a martyr's role to redeem his fellow man — in this instance freeing mankind from the scourge of a corrupt individual who threatened the stability of the social order.

At this juncture the man of reason, compelled by reason to become a man of action, displaces the romantic idealist. In *"Grim Fairy Tales"* (1949), Rex Stout would say, "We enjoy reading about people who love and hate and covet — about gluttons and martyrs, misers and sadists, whores and saints, brave men and cowards. But also, demonstrably, we enjoy reading about a man who gloriously acts and decides, with no exception and no compunction, not as his emotions brutally command, but as his reason instructs." In *In the Best Families*, the very apogee of the orbit of the Wolfe epic, Wolfe emerges as the epitome of such a man. In Greek myth the Furies, with stern, dispassionate justice, exact retribution for disruptions of the moral order. Wolfe, fully cognizant of their role, proclaims himself to be of their company, "one of the Erinyes." In this role, of course, he exactly parallels the behavior of his creator, Rex Stout, who, at the start of World War II, forsook the idyllic life he had created at High Meadow — his beautiful country estate in Danbury, Connecticut — to live in an apartment in New York City, and, as chairman of the vital Writers War Board (overseeing the activities of more than two thousand writers), engage in a campaign to bring down Adolf Hitler and his Axis allies. That campaign has been called the most successful propaganda effort ever mounted by a major nation in wartime.

During this period of service to his country and to mankind — for which he accepted neither salary nor expense money — Rex Stout stopped writing Nero Wolfe stories. This sacrifice, nonetheless, did not go uncompensated, for when he resumed writing he came to his task with a vision more broadly based and with, as well, the realization, which he had before lacked, that he should bend all his narrative efforts to writing Nero Wolfe stories. It was in these stories that his vision and his artistry came together in perfect harmony to express those views that were his contribution to the preservation of the social order and the dignity of the human condition. It may here be noted that in the Wolfe *Corpus*, even while he entertains us, Rex Stout attacks a broad spectrum of social evils: fascism, communism, McCarthyism, racism, censorship, mercantile greed, commercial radio; abuses in the law profession, in government agencies, in labor unions, in the National Association of Manufacturers, and in the publishing industry; exploitation of displaced persons; the Nixon government; and social pretense wherever encountered. This is not done with calculated didacticism but with an earnestness remote from preachment or overt chastisement that gives it a wholesome, organic relevance to the narrative at hand.

To Jacques Barzun, dean of American critics, Nero Wolfe stands as "a portrait of the Educated Man." Readers who feel intimidated by that formidable description will feel somewhat reassured, perhaps, by James M. Cain's assertion that "Nero Wolfe is one of the master creations." It was left to British novelist Kingsley Amis, however, to characterize Wolfe in terms that no true votary of detective fiction can ignore. "Wolfe," said Amis, "is the most interesting 'great detective' of them all." It cannot surprise the reader, then, to learn that newcomers to the *Corpus* have been known to put the question to long-standing Neronians, 'Are we supposed to like Nero Wolfe?' For many detective heroes the scrutiny such a question invites would be lethal. With Wolfe that is not a problem. What we know about Wolfe is what we are told by his indispensable dogsbody, Archie Goodwin, the first-person narrator of all the Nero Wolfe stories.

We see Wolfe as Archie sees him. Like Archie we can be exasperated by Wolfe's arrogance, obstinacy, and aloofness. Sometimes relations between the two men seem at the breaking point. But Archie admits that Wolfe is his "favorite fatty," and as we come to deepen our acquaintance with both men, we see why. Wolfe has none of those qualities spoken of as endearing. But he is just, sincere, humane, honest, fairminded, dignified, witty, learned, loyal, profound, and astute. Above all, he is relentlessly logical and, as a result, ultimately invincible. He grows on us with each encounter until we come to respect him and, at length, to cherish him quite as Archie does. We even become solicitous and distressed for his sake when his comforts are interfered with. Maybe his plant schedule is unreasonable and his fear of moving vehicles ludicrous. Maybe his beer drinking is excessive and his gourmet preferences (e.g., chicken fattened on blueberries) outrageous.

But we come to believe that the world owes something to this unique and heroic man and that gratifying his indulgences is a small price to pay in exchange for the services he renders to humanity. A God-the-Father figure, he is awesome but deserving of our obeisance. If he looks upon his orchids as pampered concubines that merit the attention they get because of the beauty they bestow, then we must concede that he himself should be indulged without stint because he is a superior being who, by operating mentally and morally at the level he does, exalts the human race.

Archie, on the other hand, has no trouble enlisting our loyalty, sympathy, and devotion. We find ourselves, though we know better, strangely partial to the resolute lady who showed up at a Poughkeepsie bookstore and asked for "one of those Archie books." The bookseller ruminated for a minute, then said, "You mean the Nero Wolfe books!" "Nonsense," the customer rejoined. "We know who does all the work." Even Rex Stout was able to relate to this outlook. As the saga progressed he enlarged Archie's role and, occasionally, as in *Too Many Women* (1947), kept Archie center stage while Wolfe lurked in the background. Rex's mail so consistently told him how much Archie was esteemed, he was able at last to concede, "It's Archie who really carries the stories as narrator. Whether the readers know it or not, it's Archie they really enjoy." Rex did not resent Archie's eminence. After all, though Wolfe was his achieved self, the man of intellect he became over the years, Archie was his spontaneous self, the person he most naturally was.

Many people whose judgment has to be respected have admired Archie. Agatha Christie said, "Archie is a splendid character to have invented." Leslie Charteris, creator of the Saint, maintained, "It always seemed to me that Archie was a creation worth noticing. Goodwin has his own personality, can carry out an assignment with intelligence and efficiency, and is not incapable of occasional irreverence towards some of the affectations and grandiosities of the boss. Which I found a most refreshing change from the usual formula in this genre." Charteris is referring here to the Dr. Watson stereotype, dubbed by Stephen Leacock "the Poor Sap," and by Agatha Christie (notwithstanding Captain Hastings), "the Idiot Friend," because he seems to exist either solely to reenforce the ego of the great detective with constant exclamations of astonishment, reverence, and approval, or, forgive me, to pit the reader against an observer who is stupider than he is.

When, in 1965, Jacques Barzun turned away for a moment from his duties as dean of the Columbia University Graduate School to take a close look at Archie, he came to a warmhearted conclusion: "If he had done nothing more than to create Archie Goodwin, Rex Stout would deserve the gratitude of whatever assessors watch over the prosperity of American literature. For surely Archie is one of the folk heroes in which the modern American temper can see itself transfigured."

P. G. Wodehouse was willing to go further and wasted no words in saying so. "Stout's supreme triumph," he said, "was the creation of Archie Goodwin. A Watson of some sort to tell the story is unavoidable, and the hundreds of Watsons who have appeared in print since Holmes's simply won't do. Archie is a Watson in the sense that he tells the story, but in no other way is there anything Watsonian about him. And he brings excellent comedy into the type of narrative where comedy seldom bats better than .100." Barzun is in whole-hearted agreement: "Archie is the lineal descendant of Huck Finn. Above all, he commands a turn of humor that goes to the heart of character and situation: not since Mark Twain and Mr. Dooley has the native spirit of comedy found an interpreter of equal force. Our other professional humorists of the last half century have been solid and serviceable, but their creations are not in a class with Archie."

Discussion of the *Corpus* is not ended with an acknowledgment of the merits of Wolfe and Archie. The brownstone house is itself a palpable presence in the stories, as is the intimate family group that Wolfe has gathered about him. With most detective stories our interest centers on the impact the detectives have on the crime. With the Wolfe *Corpus* our locus of interest is the impact the crime has on the detectives because it is them that we really care about. "Like P. G. Wodehouse," says Donald Westlake, "Rex Stout created a world." David Anderson, concurring, amplifies on that claim: "A writer can create a world in one novel — as Rex Stout did in *Fer-de-Lance* — but a world developed and established over seventy-two tales and forty-two years becomes more than a fictive world — it becomes a fictive home."

In addition to those residing in the brownstone with Wolfe — Archie; Fritz Brenner, Swiss chef and general factotum; and Theodore Horstmann, who tends the orchids — Wolfe's intimate world includes also his "professional family," as Fred Durkin calls it, which, in addition to Fred, includes Saul Panzer, Orrie Cather, Johnny Keems (slain in the line of duty), and Bill Gore (dropped because he bored his creator). These are the operatives, men of varying excellence, who along with Theodolinda Bonner and Sally Colt, supplement Archie when need arises. By extension we can add three more to this number, newsman Lon Cohen, Lily Rowan, Archie's girlfriend — "I would tackle a tiger bare-handed to save her from harm," Rex told me when a reader had the consummate nerve to propose that he should kill her off — and Inspector L. T. Cramer who, occasionally at least, is cordially received at West Thirty-fifth Street, though by no means always. In their supportive roles, as the bulwark that helps to hold off the menacing forces of the world beyond the brownstone, these individuals make Wolfe's edenic haven seem more probable and more possible.

Archie, who sometimes indiscreetly boasts that Wolfe needs him to goad him into action — rather like a mahout prodding an elephant — on occasion has been described as Wolfe's tinderbox. But if this is so, then Inspector Cramer is the bellows that quickens the flame. Quite commonly in detective fiction, when the detective is a private investigator, his efficiency is underscored by emphasizing the incompetence and ineptitude of the police. Rex Stout avoids that snare. Lieutenant Rowcliff is despised, of course, and his shortcomings stressed over many years till finally he receives his comeuppance in the penultimate Nero Wolfe novel, *Please Pass the Guilt* (1973). Since George Rowcliff was modeled on a naval officer under whom Rex Stout served in 1905-1906 when he was pay yeoman on Theodore Roosevelt's presidential yacht, the officer must have left deep wounds. But Sergeant Purley Stebbins and Cramer are portrayed with consideration. In fact, one of Rex Stout's favorite scenes in the *Corpus* came in *The Doorbell Rang* (1965), when Cramer, meeting secretly with Archie to give him some background on the case they were working on, brought with him a carton of milk for Archie since he knew that that was Archie's preferred beverage. "I think I wrote that very well," Rex told me, "I think that's done just the way such an episode should be done." Rex resented any suggestion that he came down hard on the police in the Wolfe *Corpus*. Indeed, he thought it a fine endorsement of the democratic system that, in his books, he showed that private investigators could disagree with the police now and again yet not be prevented from carrying on independently of them — a situation that would not have been conceivable in a totalitarian state. Indeed, Rex was delighted when he learned that readers in the Soviet Union were impressed that Rex Stout, in *The Doorbell Rang*, could take on J. Edgar Hoover himself and not be imprisoned or silenced.

Back in the 1950s when a college president and his wife were disembarking from a cab on West Thirty-seventh Street in New York City, the lady said to her husband, "Isn't this where Nero Wolfe lives?" Before he could answer, the shocked cabbie intervened. "Oh, no," he said. "Wolfe lives on West Thirty-fifth Street." The cabbie was justified in his indignation for, after all, he had a right to expect this fact to be common knowledge. In the fifty years that have elapsed since *Fer-de-Lance* was first published, the Nero Wolfe stories have been translated into twenty-seven languages and have sold, in all editions, more than one hundred million copies. *The London Times* has reported that of all the writers who ever wrote in English the two who sell best behind the Iron Curtain now are Agatha Christie and Rex Stout. What is even more remarkable, Stout is available there only in contraband editions. "Do not mail me any of Stout's books," a Prague editor wrote to me sadly, "because I would not be allowed to have them."

During World War II, FDR sometimes read the Wolfe stories to relax from the burdens of office. Dwight D. Eisenhower read *Prisoner's Base* (1952) while recovering from a heart attack during his first term as president. In England, Anthony Eden, as prime minister of Great Britain, devoured the novels with enthusiasm. Former French president Giscard d'Estaing, more recently, confessed that Nero Wolfe was his favorite reading. John Cardinal Wright, a member of the Vatican Curia, liked the stories well enough to write Rex Stout a fan letter. William Faulkner quoted Nero Wolfe in his Nobel Prize acceptance speech. John Steinbeck wrote a poem about Wolfe and Archie. Moss Hart schemed to write a play about them. The Vermont Symphony Orchestra, in the dead of winter, premiered a "Wolfe and Archie Overture." Ian Fleming introduced Nero Wolfe into a James Bond thriller and asserted that Stout's was "one of the most civilized minds ever to concern itself with detective fiction." He asked Rex to collaborate with him on a Wolfe and Bond novel. "No," said Rex, "Bond would get the girl. Archie wouldn't like that."

Other admirers of the Wolfe *Corpus* whom Stout sometimes heard from included Hubert Humphrey, Graham Greene, Georges Simenon, Marlene Dietrich, T. E. Lawrence (Lawrence of Arabia), Alfred Lunt and Lynn Fontanne, Aldous Huxley, J. B. Priestley, Henry Miller, Norman Cousins, Richard Rodgers, Oscar Hammerstein II, Bertrand Russell, Norbert Wiener, Robert Parker, John Wayne, Robert Penn Warren, Henry Morgan, Louis Untermeyer, Mary Stewart, Ellery Queen, Sir Hugh Greene, Joseph Wood Krutch, Marian Anderson, Havelock Ellis, Karl Menninger, Jerome Weidman, Clifton Fadiman, Herblock, and the Maharajah of Indore. No less appreciated were the letters he had from shopgirls, cowhands, college boys, soldiers, switchboard operators, housewives, lawyers, doctors, professors, scientists (including Lew Kowarski, senior physicist at the European Center for Nuclear Research), and men and women in prison.

Eric Ambler wrote: "Those who like the detective story have

special reason to be grateful to Rex Stout because a considerable body of work such as his, with its consistent ingenuity and fine craftsmanship, raises the whole standard of the genre a further notch above the mundane." Ross Macdonald carried praise a step further: "Rex Stout is one of the half dozen major figures in the development of the American detective novel. With great wit and cunning, he devised a form which combined the traditional values of Sherlock Holmes and the English school with the fast-moving vernacular narrative of Dashiell Hammett." Mark Van Doren, with glorious abandon, added this accolade: "Rex is a perfect writer — economical, rapid, free of cliché, epigrammatic, intelligent, charming. What else? That's enough." Lawrence Block sums up, not without a note of anguish: "I've found Rex Stout books about Nero Wolfe endlessly rereadable. There's nothing ordinary about Wolfe and it's not only his corpulence that makes him larger than life. Ordinary? Scarcely that. But so real that I sometimes have to remind myself that Wolfe and Goodwin are the creations of a writer's mind, that no matter how many doorbells I ring in the West Thirties, I'll never find the right house." As realists we should agree with him. But can we be sure?

The death of Rex Stout, on October 27, 1975, was front-page news in *The New York Times*. That autumn fifty-seven Nero Wolfe books were in print, more books than any other living American writer had available at the time. On the *"Evening News,"* Harry Reasoner told an ABC-TV audience, "The odds are over-whelming that when historians look at the bright blue late October of 1975 the only thing they will keep about the twenty-seventh is that it was the day Rex Stout died. Rex Stout was a lot of things during his eighty-eight years, but the main thing he was was the writer of seventy-two mysteries about Nero Wolfe and Archie Goodwin. A lot of more pretentious writers have less claim on our culture and our allegiance." *The Sunday London Times* marked Rex's death with "Ave Atque Vale," a thirty-six line elegy by Edmund Crispin, author and composer.

To those who knew Rex, and Wolfe, and Archie, this recognition came as no surprise. They were merely getting their due.

Rex Stout said once that he was curious to know "what, of course, I'll never know," that is, how Nero Wolfe would be looked on a century hence, if remembered at all. He had no cause for anxiety. Nearly a decade after his death the Wolfe *Corpus* still is selling briskly. The Wolfe Pack, called into existence by admiring fans, has members in every corner of the globe. There is a Wolfe Pack *Gazette* and a *Rex Stout Newsletter*, both quarterlies. More than a hundred articles have been written about the *Corpus*, and seven books. Another three books are in progress. Mia Gerhardt, a professor at the University of Utrecht (in the Netherlands), has drawn a favorable comparison between Quixote and Wolfe and Panza and Archie. Wolfe's likeness has appeared on postage stamps in Nicaragua and the Republic of San Marino. The Authors League has established a Rex Stout Award; the Wolfe Pack, a Nero Award. Wolfe, who has appeared in two Hollywood movies and three radio serials in the past, has been the subject of a TV movie, based on *The Doorbell Rang*, and two TV series, one in the U.S., the other in Italy. He has had an orchid named after him. And a Yale man who, on a visit to London, shouted the name Nero Wolfe at Paddington Station, found himself besieged by eager admirers of the brainy sleuth. Never doubt it. At fifty Wolfe and Archie are alive and well.

The Wolfe *Corpus* opens in June 1933 and carries through to November 1974. Rex Stout was forty-seven when he wrote *Fer-de-Lance* and eighty-eight when he wrote *A Family Affair*. When, at the behest of publisher John Farrar, he wrote *Fer-de-Lance* he did not foresee that so many stories would follow. What would he have said in 1934 had someone given him a glimpse of the labors that lay ahead of him? "Nuts!" he told me. Nonetheless, though the events in each story always correspond to the year in which it was written, and often to the very days, Rex Stout prudently kept Wolfe and Archie at the same ages they were when he introduced them in *Fer-de-Lance* (fifty-eight and thirty-four), almost as though he anticipated the difficulty of having to deal with a Nero Wolfe who would be ninety-nine in 1974 and an

Archie who would be (we shudder at the thought), seventy-five. He believed it would be easier for him to adopt the persona of a man thirty-four, through the medium of Archie, than to deal with aged heroes. And this, though he admitted at the end that the effort was taking an increasing lot out of him, he was able to do. Incredibly, when he wrote *A Family Affair*, he still caught to perfection, in Archie's breezy style, the spirit of a man of thirty-four. Not for him Agatha Christie's dilemma of having a centenarian Hercule Poirot doing his final bit of detecting from a wheelchair. When Rex finished *A Family Affair*, he had a stroke from which he did not recover. But he had done what he had set out to do, without a hitch, and to him that was all that mattered.

While it is possible to pick up with the Wolfe *Corpus* at any point and to read the stories in any sequence, since, like a cask, each narrative rests on its own bottom, something is to be gained from reading them in chronological order on a second if not a first reading. In addition to the mounting sophistication that comes with the author's expanding social and ethical vision, the characters themselves show change and growth. At the outset Archie is somewhat rawboned and rough-edged, as befits a youth not so many years off the farm at Chillicothe, Ohio. After prolonged association with Wolfe — a true Renaissance man — Archie sheds the more disagreeable qualities that link him to detective fiction's hard-boiled tradition. Wolfe, for his part, enters into a more paternal relationship with Archie, a relationship of the kind that emerges when a grown son succeeds to a condition of friendship with a father who respects him for his maturity and achievements. Most of all, a chronological reading brings us to a full comprehension of Wolfe's success in coming to terms, despite his romantic ideals, with the reality of the world he lives in.

In *The Honorary Consul*, Graham Greene speaks of the comfort to be had from a detective story: "The story of a dream world where justice is always done." At the end of *A Family Affair*, the front door of the brownstone is shattered — not left merely ajar as it was in *In the Best Families* (which novel readily pairs with this one as the titles invite us to notice), but utterly demolished — reminding Wolfe that our responsibilities carry beyond our own threshold and there is no denying that fact. We may try to shut out the reality of evil in our own lives, to create a paradise from which evil is forever excluded. Yet in the end it will seek us out. Wolfe does not flinch from this truth. He does his duty and cleans his own house. But something is changed for good and always. He is compelled to realize that we cannot isolate ourselves from the rest of mankind — we are all members, one of another, mutually interdependent. He knows that the tide of chaos has reached his doors. Years before he had said, "For the sake of truth and justice we must be prepared to receive the thorn." When the thorn is offered now, he does not refuse it.

We need not suppose, however, that Wolfe, in confronting reality, abandoned his faith in an ordered universe. Rex Stout, planning a further Nero Wolfe story at the time of his death, last spoke of Wolfe contentedly rereading Jane Austen's *Emma*, one of Rex's own favorites. Emma Woodhouse's follies and her way of dealing with them remind us that decency and honor, no matter how severely besieged, may emerge strengthened and triumphant if we do not abandon faith in mankind's basic decency, for the human spirit is, after all, touched by the attar of divinity.

When, toward the close of his life, Rex Stout was asked if he had plans to send Wolfe to his grave, even as Agatha Christie had done unto Poirot, and Doyle sought to do with Holmes, Rex Stout cocked one eyebrow (a talent he shared in common with Archie), and said, "I hope he lives forever!" We have no cause to think that that hope will not be met.

Indeed, new strength constantly is being added to the ranks of those who echo Phyllis McGinley's rallying refrain:

Come, mark them down with a big black zero
Who don't love Archie, Rex, and Nero.

REX STOUT AND HIS TWO LIVES

by Jacques Barzun

*(An after-dinner talk given December 5th, 1981,
at The Wolfe Pack Black Orchid Banquet)*

LADIES AND GENTLEMEN — or perhaps I should say: Fellow
Neronians: It is a honor to be here, not solely as an after-dinner
speaker, but simply as one of you. I only wish that circumstances
had not kept this pleasure from me until tonight. For I have
rejoiced in the existence of this Society from the start. It is important that there should be a collection of watchdogs — watch-
wolves — to keep guard over the fame and right significance of
Nero and Archie.

Fame is, of course, hard to control. When the TV series about
our two friends [*The earlier series starring William Conrad — MK*]
was on the air, the only way I could express my irritation — my
indignation — was to turn off the set. The next week I turned it on
once more — in hopes. But there they were again: Nero looking
and talking like a stingy landlord, Archie like an ivy-league
junior executive. And the house! The house on West 35th Street,
resembling, inside, the premises of an expensive fortuneteller
and, outside, the facade of a discreet private — er — hotel. There
comes Inspector Cramer, seeming both embarrassed and petu-
lant and making willowy movements with his torso. The stories
themselves were feeble — no bursts of impatience or anger, let

alone wit and repartee. Only the clients looked the part and behaved in keeping.

I resolved that if these travesties start up again, I shall see if the leaders of this group will organize a mass picketing of the broadcasting station, or better: a Wolfe-in at the studio.

The point of dwelling on something best forgotten is that I find in this perversion of Rex Stout's creation a sign of our general, national loss of common sense and mental vigor. What is marvelous about Nero and Archie is that together they make up the ideal American — the man or woman who can think straight and enjoy thinking, while pursuing practical ends with a social conscience.

And our two heros do this with humor and irony. They play up to an image of themselves as part of a perpetual domestic comedy — Nero the idle, self-indulgent highbrow; Archie the lowbrow always looking out for No. 1. They keep up the joke for their amusement and ours, and that, too, is an American tradition. I remember several arguments about it with my old friend C. P. Snow and his wife Pamela Hansford Johnson, the novelist. They liked the Wolfe tales and took Nero at face value, which was not enough. They disliked Archie intensely, thought him crude and often stupid; they believed he was a sop to the low tastes of the American reader. When I told them that Archie was a great character, the literary descendant of Huckleberry Finn, they tried hard but could not understand what I meant.

It wasn't because they were English that they missed the point. As we've seen, the master minds of television also got it wrong; and earlier, Alexander Woolcott (as you all know) had the notion that he was the model for Nero Wolfe. The only likeness between those two was their measurement around the waist.

What is missing in all these judgments is the simple idea that a person can combine high intelligence with common habits and common speech, and even with vulgar tastes. This blend was the very essence of Rex Stout himself. Like Mark Twain he led his life on two levels, by choice, and also as a product of his characteristically American experience, his forty menial or manual jobs before he became a literary man. In that final role, he endowed his two heros with the same qualities.

But it won't do to take this democratic mix as predictable: you can't tell what Nero or Archie will like or despise. And it won't do to be literal. In an interview with Rex by Michael Murray, an admirer who is also a distinguished musician, Rex answered a question about the way he composed at the typewriter — straight off, without revising or even rereading: "It's because I have a neat mind and the soul of a bookkeeper." What a wonderful misstatement! Those of us who write painfully and revise up to eight or ten times have met plenty of neat minds and a few bookkeepers, but none with the ability to knock off a Wolfean adventure so effortlessly and with such art in plotting, such variety and precision of language.

Seeing Rex perform at committee meetings, as I had the privilege of doing for some ten years at the Authors' League, was a revelation of the same improvisatory genius. He balanced principle with practice, argument with diplomacy: it was Nero conducting one of his detective seminars in the big room and getting his man by the application of sheer intelligence.

It is obvious that this Society is following in the footsteps of the three men it has chosen to celebrate. As people concerned with the ideas and opinions found in the written works and the character of their creator, while also relishing the down-to-earth details peculiar to the detective genre, we emulate Rex. We follow him also in his high regard for the word. He had little or none for music, and we gave evidence earlier this evening that we feel exactly as he did. [*A reference to the song parodies at Pack banquets that each table of diners prepares and presents (sing not being le mot juste) a cappella. — MK*]

But first and last we are pedants — pedants like Nero pontificating and burning the pages of the Webster III Dictionary; like Archie giving us points on ballistics or female beauty; and like Rex himself lecturing on cooking and gardening. No need to apologize for our attitude in such pleasant occupations; for as somebody has well said: "My pedantry is your scholarship, his accuracy, her good education, and the other fellow's ignorance."

If anybody objects, we reply that unlike many other groups, we are a pack with a mind of its own.

A CHRONOLOGY OF THE NERO WOLFE MYSTERIES

Adapted from a Compilation
by Stephen F. Schultheis

[*Non-Neronian mysteries are included; I have indicated characters in them from the Wolfe tales, as well as the Tecumseh Fox novels, one of which Rex Stout rewrote and made into a Nero Wolfe story.* — MK]

Date events occurred	Book or novelette (" ") title	1st publication
June 1933	*Fer-de-Lance*	1934
November 1934	*The League of Frightened Men*	1935
October 1935	*The Rubber Band* (Alternate title: To Kill Again)	1936
March-April 1936	*The Red Box*	1937
September 1936	*The Hand in the Glove* (*Crime on Her Hands*) NON-WOLFE: Dol Bonner	1937
April 1937	*Too Many Cooks*	1938
July 1937	*Red Threads* NON-WOLFE: Inspector Cramer	1939
September 1937	*Some Buried Caesar* (*The Red Bull*)	1939

June 1938	*Mountain Cat* (*The Mountain Cat Murders*) NON-WOLFE	1939
November 1938	*Over My Dead Body*	1940
July 1939	*Where There's a Will*	1940
Summer 1939	*Double for Death* NON-WOLFE: Tecumseh Fox	1939
November 1939	*Bad for Business* NON-WOLFE: Tecumseh Fox [*Rewritten by Stout as the 1ˢᵗ Nero Wolfe* **short story,** "Bitter End," *published in the posthumous* *Death Times Three.*]	1940
March 1940	*The Broken Vase* NON-WOLFE: Tecumseh Fox	1941
September 1940	*Alphabet Hicks* (*The Sound of Murder*) NON-WOLFE	1941
November 1940 (?)	"Bitter End" [in: *The American Magazine*, later reprinted in *Corsage* and *Death Times Three* — MK]	1940
March 1941	"Black Orchids"	1942
August 1941	"Cordially Invited to Meet Death" (in: *Black Orchids*)	1942
March 1942	*Not Quite Dead Enough*	1944
August 1943	"Booby Trap" (in: *Curtains for Three*)	1944
May 1944	"Help Wanted: Male" (in: *Trouble in Triplicate*)	1949
October 1944	"Instead of Evidence" (in: *Trouble in Triplicate*)	1949

October 1944	"Bullet for One" (in: *Curtains for Three*)	1950
March-April 1945	*The Silent Speaker*	1946
October 1946	"Before I Die" (in: *Trouble in Triplicate*) 1949	
March-April 1947	*Too Many Women*	1947
June 1947	"Man Alive" (in: *Three Doors to Death*) 1950	
March-April 1948	*And Be a Villain* (*More Deaths than One*) 1948 [1st Arnold Zeck case — MK]	
July 1948	"Omit Flowers" (in: *Three Doors to Death*)	1950
December 1948	"Door to Death" (in: *Three Doors to Death*)	1950
June 1949	*The Second Confession* [2nd Arnold Zeck case — MK]	1949
August 1949	"The Gun with Wings" (in: *Curtains for Three*)	1950
Fall 1949	"The Cop Killer" (in: *Triple Jeopardy*)	1952
March 1950	"Disguise for Murder" (in: *Curtains for Three*)	1950
April-Sept. 1950	*In the Best Families* (*Even in the Best Families*) [3rd and final Arnold Zeck case — MK]	1950
Winter 1950	"The Squirt and the Monkey" (in: *Triple Jeopardy*)	1952
December 1950	"Christmas Party" (in: *And Four to Go*) 1958	
Jan.-March 1951	*Murder by the Book*	1951
July-August 1951	"Home to Roost" (in: *Triple Jeopardy*)	1952

October 1951	"This Won't Kill You" (in: *Three Men Out*)	1954
June 1952	*Prisoner's Base (Out Goes She)*	1952
Fall 1952	"Invitation to Murder" (in: *Three Men Out*)	1954
May 1953	*The Golden Spiders*	1953
Fall 1953	"The Zero Clue" (in: *Three Men Out*)	1954
March-April 1954	*The Black Mountain*	1954
May 1954	"When a Man Murders" (in: *Three Witnesses*)	1956
September 1954	"The Next Witness" (in: *Three Witnesses*)	1956
Fall 1954	"Die Like a Dog" (in: *Three Witnesses)*	1956
April 1955	*Before Midnight*	1955
August 1955	"A Window for Death" (in: *Three for the Chair*)	1957
Fall 1955	"Immune to Murder" (in: *Three for the Chair*)	1957
January 1956	"Too Many Detectives" (in: *Three for the Chair*)	1957
March-April 1956	"Easter Parade" (in: *And Four to Go*)	1958
April 1956	*Might as Well Be Dead*	1956
May-June 1957	*If Death Ever Slept*	1957
July 1957	"Fourth of July Picnic"	1958
Summer 1957	"Murder Is No Joke" (in: *And Four to Go*) [A variant version, "Frame-Up for Murder," is in *Death Times Three*, 1985 — MK]	1958
March 1958	*Champagne for One*	1958

April 1958	"Poison a la Carte" (in: *Three at Wolfe's Door*)	1960
January 1959	"Eeny Meeny Murder Mo" (in: *Homicide Trinity*)	1962
May-June 1959	Plot It Yourself	1959
September 1959	"Method Three for Murder" (in: *Three at Wolfe's Door*)	1960
October 1959	"The Rodeo Murder" (in: *Three at Wolfe's Door*)	1960
January 1960	"Death of a Demon" (in: *Homicide Trinity*)	1962
May 1960	*Too Many Clients*	1960
December 1960	"Kill Now — Pay Later" (in: *Trio for Blunt Instruments*)	1964
Winter 1960/1961	"Counterfeit for Murder" (in: *Homicide Trinity*) [A revision, "Assault on a Brownstone," was to appear in *Death Times Three* (1958), but the familiar text was erroneously used instead. — MK]	1962
April-May 1961	*The Final Deduction*	1961
September 1961	"Murder Is Corny" (in: *Trio for Blunt Instruments*)	1964
February 1962	*Gambit*	1962
June-July 1962	*The Mother Hunt*	1963
August 1962	"Blood Will Tell" (in: *Trio for Blunt Instruments*)	1964
September 1963 (1963)	"Why Nero Wolfe Likes Orchids" [Though not a mystery, this is Archie's amusing speculation on Wolfe's love of orchids. It first appeared in the September	1963

15, 1963, issue of *Life* and was reprinted in *Corsage* (1977) — MK]

Feb.-March 1964	*A Right to Die*	1964
January 1965	*The Doorbell Rang*	1965
Jan.-Feb. 1966	*Death of a Doxy*	1966
Aug.-Sept. 1967	*The Father Hunt*	1968
August 1968	*Death of a Dude*	1969
Summer 1969	*Please Pass the Guilt*	1973
October 1974	*A Family Affair*	1975

WORKING WITH REX STOUT

by Barbara Benjamin

(This speech was presented at the December 7, 2003,
Black Orchid Banquet.)

HOW WONDERFUL it is that the memory of Rex Stout and the kind of special human being he was is being kept alive by all of you. It goes without saying that the memory of Rex Stout keeps Nero Wolfe and Archie alive as well.

I thank you for inviting me tonight. However, I want you to know this was not *my* idea. If my aging memory of the time I spent working for Rex Stout seems to be somewhat slimmer than anticipated, I urge you to blame my dear friend and neighbor Mike Schwartz. He can be very, very persuasive. He is the person to whom you can complain. Actually, if the truth be known, I blackmailed Mike by telling him I would not come tonight unless he and his wife Judy made a contribution to a group I'm involved with that's working to prevent the environmental destruction of our hometown, White Plains. I like to think they caved in, but I feel certain they would have made the contribution, anyway.

If anyone had told me, well over fifty years ago, that the secretarial job I held at the time would lead to my appearance here tonight, I would have insisted they get some psychiatric help in a big hurry. But here I am, and I confess it's kind of fun to reminisce out loud about my adventures during that period of my life. Perhaps it's an exaggeration to call my experiences adventures, but I was very young at the time, and they seemed adventurous to me.

To talk about Rex Stout without providing a picture of the world as it was in the forties would be to discuss him in a one dimensional vacuum without giving appropriate weight to his remarkable leadership and the passion he had for what he believed to be the only possible road to universal humanity.

I had absolutely no idea who Rex Stout was when I started my job, and I had never read a Nero Wolfe mystery. But even as I became a Nero Wolfe fan and got to know Rex Stout, it was not until many years later that I fully realized what an unusual person he truly was. At the time I worked for him I was mostly struck by his incredible fund of knowledge; his wonderful sense of humor; his intimidating ability to spot poor grammar and mis-spelled words; his genuine respect for women even before the women's movement; his mind-boggling acquaintance with what seemed to be every living famous writer, everyone in the New York world of theatre, politicians from the President on down, and every liberal I had ever heard of and then some. However, the full extent of his passion, the degree to which he dedicated his life to the causes he believed in, and the high respect with which he was regarded by those who knew him were things of which I was unaware.

Earlier today I was watching the news on television and it reminded me of how incredibly different the world was during World War II. Of course we didn't have television; plans to go to war were not announced beforehand; it never occurred to anyone we would start a war or that the government would allow, and even encourage, public discussion of where and how we would strike. Young men in college were not exempt from the draft, and once drafted and sent overseas, their only way to com-municate with worried family was by sending slow mail that was censored by the army. In addition, we had Jim Crow units and open bigotry against blacks and Jews. Much as I viewed the Roosevelts in very positive terms — particularly Eleanor — it was no secret that the president was anti-Semitic. The only visual view of war was out-of-date newsreels shown in movie theatres and the limited number of pictures printed in the papers.

Bombers could not fly the Atlantic and return home safely, so although we had blackout drills in New York City, we really felt completely safe.

It was into this ridiculously complacent society that accepted bigotry and a sense of superiority and safety that Rex Stout marched with all his verbal guns blazing.

If you want to know how the Writers' War Board came into existence and what it accomplished, I recommend you read the McAleer book. But I will tell you that the writers Rex Stout persuaded to work with the Writers' War Board made the very first genuine and successful effort to remove negative stereotypes from the media: newspapers, magazines, books, and radio. And after the war, when Rex Stout tried to keep the organization going under the new name of Writers' Board, the effort was continued.

Having married my handsome uniformed hero at the ripe old age of nineteen (not the least bit unusual in those days), I had switched from being a full-time day student at NYU to nighttime classes and was looking for a job. Since I was now a married woman, I did not want my family to continue to give me an allowance, particularly since I was still living at home rent-free. I had already had one dreadful, boring job where I worked five and one-half days for $30 a week. Work in the commercial world was something I decided I did not want to do. Not-for-profit seemed more appealing. Fortunately a friend of my mother's knew of someone at the American Jewish Committee who was looking for a secretary. So, I applied for the job and was hired. Heaven! It was only five days a week and the salary was $35 a week. Although my boss Selma Hirsch was indeed an employee of the AJC, her assignment was to work for Rex Stout doing public relations at the Writers' War Board. So now you know. I'm here under a somewhat false pretense. I did not start out as Rex Stout's secretary.

We were a very small office and everyone who worked there simply took care of what needed to be done, regardless of our specific assignment. The world of office work was as different then as was the world outside the office. We did not have electric typewriters, computers with spell check, copy or fax machines, not even telephone-answering machines or call forwarding. We took dictation in shorthand, made copies with carbon paper or occasionally a mimeograph machine, and made certain there was always someone present to answer the phone.

When I arrived at the office on my first day of work, neither Selma Hirsch nor Rex Stout was in yet. Even before I had taken my coat off, the phone in my office rang. Although I had no idea who was calling the voice at the other end of the phone had an eerily familiar ring to it. I asked if the caller would like to leave a message and he said, "Yes, please tell Mrs. Hirsch that Melvyn Douglas called and would she please call me back. She has my number." There was a moment of dead silence on my part and then, with remarkable maturity and sophistication, I said, "Oh, oh, oh, OH, yes, of course, Mr. Douglas, I'll be absolutely certain to give her the message just the very first minute she comes in." This was followed by a moment of silence on his part (it seemed like a million years) and then he said soothingly, "That will be just fine. Thank you." And hung up. I could barely breathe. Melvyn Douglas was one of my very favorite movie actors, not as a romantic figure, but rather because of his remarkable resemblance to my father. It strikes me as fortunate I didn't tell him that at the time.

The interesting thing about Melvyn Douglas as representative of the kind of people who were involved with the WWB was that he was married to wonderfully liberal Helen Gahagan Douglas. Years later, in a campaign for a California seat in the House, her opponent, an unknown new politician, became famous for his despicable, nasty, lying campaign against her when such campaigns were very, very rare. His name was Richard Nixon.

Sometime later I had another experience I have never forgotten. Since we lacked fax machines, Rex Stout asked me to take a manuscript to Clifton Fadiman, moderator of the top-10 radio hit *Information Please*, who lived in midtown and not very far away. He lived on an upper floor of a brownstone. I rang the bell downstairs and Fadiman buzzed me in. Then I took the elevator up to his apartment, totally unprepared for what awaited me. There were two apartments on the floor and in front of the open door to one apartment stood Clifton Fadiman wearing nothing at all except his undershorts. I did the best I could not to allow my reaction of horror to show on my face, but I could feel it getting very red. He greeted me cordially and invited me in. To be perfectly honest, I was scared to death, but I couldn't figure out any polite way to refuse. Facing the front door as I entered was a couch with a bed pillow at one end and a floor-model sun lamp behind it. Obviously Fadiman had been getting a winter suntan, a fact that was, at most, only moderately reassuring. The problem I had was that for the time I was in the apartment, I simply could not figure out where to look because I was too embarrassed to look at Fadiman. I shook for days after, but I never mentioned it to Rex Stout.

Much of the work Rex Stout did with the members of the Board was done at lunch, Algonquin-style, so it was not a bit unusual for him to be gone for a very long time in the middle of the day. On one occasion he was gone for an unusually long time. To our absolute amazement, the Rex Stout who returned to the office did not look one bit like the Rex Stout who had left for lunch. He never said one single word about his change in appearance, and neither did we. But it took us a very long time to get used to Rex Stout without white hair and a white beard. He had dyed them while he was out for lunch!

We were all the recipients of his very generous nature. He often brought us such things as great big, gorgeous, delicious peaches and other food he had grown, and one year for Christmas he gave us house seats for one of the great musicals that was on Broadway at the time.

The summer after the war was over, while the Board members were trying to decide how to keep the organization going, they concluded they should keep the office open during the summer and have someone there to answer the phone and mail. I accepted the job, lonely through I knew it would be, and was given a small petty cash fund to use for postage or whatever. About halfway through the summer, as I was running low on cash, I put together a report for Rex Stout with all of my carefully collected receipts for Scotch tape and the like because I needed to replace the $20 or so I had spent. The response was typical Stout. "Obviously," he wrote, "you think I don't trust you. I do. I neither need nor wish to have receipts of any kind. Just tell me how much money you need and I'll send it."

It saddens me that Rex Stout never knew that eventually I became a cookbook writer and editor. I know it would have delighted him.

And finally, I wanted to make some observations about some of the ways in which Rex Stout appears, or does not appear, in the characters of Nero Wolfe and Archie Goodwin. And although it may not be the most prudent thing for me to do, I somehow feel obligated, in memory of Rex Stout, to relate those characteristics to the television series. If my remarks disturb some of you I would hope that you empty your coffee cups before you throw them at me.

Let me begin by referring to an earlier comment I made regarding Rex Stout's rigid adherence to proper English. Several weeks ago I heard a character talking to Archie in the television series. I don't remember the exact sentence, but I still cringe at the grammar. The essence of what she said was, "They told Carlos and I." It would seem there is absolutely no one in the entire television industry — writers, actors, producers, or anyone else — who knows how to speak or write proper English. But whatever gross grammatical errors are made on other programs, it is unthinkable that Rex Stout would ever, ever have written an ungrammatical sentence.

A big difference between Rex Stout and Nero Wolfe lies in Nero Wolfe's attitude toward women. In this respect it is Archie who is Rex Stout. Archie had a genuine respect for women, a good relationship with a longtime female friend (at least in the books), and a healthy enjoyment observing attractive women.

Archie is never callow or disrespectful of women in any way. Wolfe, on the other hand is terrified of women, which Rex Stout certainly was not. The Wolfe that Rex Stout created would never have physically grappled with a woman in his office as he did on television recently. Wolfe did not even want to shake hands with a woman.

Although Rex Stout was very casual in dress, his characters were not. In this respect, Rex Stout would never have had Wolfe wear a ridiculous outfit out of the office as he did when he wore a knit cap in the country.

I was delighted to find the flapper era gone from the introduction when I saw the last show. It was hopelessly inappropriate. I may be wrong, but I think only one Nero Wolfe book was written in the twenties. The thirties were not the flapper era, nor were the forties or fifties.

Good manners were important to Rex Stout and historically, polite men never wore hats indoors when I was growing up. They took them off to greet a lady, in elevators, and on every indoor occasion. And I never saw any well-dressed man wearing brown and white shoes with a business suit. Rex Stout would have cringed.

Archie, like Rex Stout, was highly intelligent, and in no way a shallow "gofer." It was his sophistication and intelligence that were indispensable to Wolfe. And although Archie was perfectly willing to enjoy a hamburger now and then, he had a serious appreciation for good food and was quite knowledgeable on the subject.

I cannot imagine a time when Archie would have allowed Cramer to barge in on Wolfe while he was eating. In the event Archie could not stop him, Wolfe would never have continued to eat while he debated with Cramer. Nor can I imagine a time when Archie would open the front door without looking through a peephole to see who was on the other side of the door.

I often found Wolfe portrayed as a childish fool in spite of the fact that he was never portrayed that way by Rex Stout. He was difficult and stubborn. But he was not churlish. He never made a fool of himself. And Archie was a thoroughly grown-up man, and not a flippant jerk.

It was rare that I watched Nero Wolfe on television as it makes me sad. I was looking forward to the series. But I truly cringe at what I feel Rex Stout's opinion of the television portrayal of his beloved characters turned out to be. They completely lack the depth of their creator.

It's been fun to be here tonight and, if you have any questions, I'll be happy to answer them if I can.

Question: Ms. Benjamin, did Rex Stout base Archie's extraordinary secretarial skills on your talents?

Answer: No!

A MEETING OF MINDS

by Marion S. Wilcox

NOTE: *Marion Wilcox is too modest to admit it, but she was Rex Stout's quintessential fan. Of the thousands of readers who wrote to Rex, Marion was singled out by Rex for a correspondence that lasted twenty years and was broken only by his death.*
— John McAleer

WHEN IN April, 1955, I offered to write to Rex Stout to ask for an autographed copy of one of his books for a scholarship fund auction sponsored by an organization I belonged to in Syracuse, New York, I had no idea what it would lead to.

By that time, I had been reading detective fiction for several years. Although I am not sure now what book initiated this interest, I am sure Rex Stout had by then become my favorite author. So much so that at the end of the begging letter (on the reverse side, actually) I added a postscript about my mental image of the layout of the West 35th Street premises.

I said I hoped he wouldn't mind, but I had been picturing the office on the right side of the house upon entering from the front, with the dining room on the left. By the time I read one of the earlier books containing his version of the layout it was too late; it would have meant a complete rearrangement of my thinking and I preferred to keep the famous establishment just as I had so firmly engraved it in my mind.

His prompt and delightful answer contained one sentence:

"It's a pleasure to send a book for your auction, but don't you get started rearranging the Wolfe premises or you'll get me all confused."

Ten years later he sent me a printed layout of his own version of the first floor. In an interview published in *P.S.* in August 1966, Rex explained why. Asked the question: "Have you ever made a sketch of Nero's house?" he answered:

"I had to make a sketch of the ground floor because I got so many requests from people who asked exactly what the make-up of the ground floor was. I made up the sketch not for myself, but so that I could have lots of copies made. When anybody writes and asks me about the layout, instead of writing them a letter, I can just send them one of these things."

Apparently he had not forgotten my original comments because I, too, received a copy of the official floor plan with a message on the bottom: "for the benevolent purpose of confusing Marion Wilcox, Rex Stout, 12/4/65." I learned later that I am not the only reader who has a mirror image of the floor plan of the brownstone. Others who own up to this interesting heresy are Henry Morgan, Lawrence Brooks, and Rex's (late) sister, Ruth Stout.

The book for the auction was *The Black Mountain*, the first of only two books in my collection of autographed books that do not have a personal touch, the other being *Might as Well Be Dead*, contributed to the next year's auction. How could Rex know for sure who the highest bidder would be?

When I thanked Rex for his first gift, I reported at length on what I called "a little aftermath." This was a luncheon at Rita Hennessey's home in Syracuse, at which Frannie Tucker, Katherine Sullivan, and I introduced our hostess to the Wolfe household. We became founding members of the Syracuse Rex Stout Fan Club. In my letter I wrote, "We probably won't have any set pattern for procedure. As Frannie said, 'What other purpose than just to admire the creator of Nero Wolfe?' I asked if he had any suggestions for the SRSFC, and, most impertinently, if he thought it would be helpful if we knew a little bit more about him as a person. I even had the temerity to tell this dear man that I thought he was distinguished in appearance with his goatee and

I thought it would be fun to have one of his photographs.

All these years later, I cannot imagine myself doing this, but he must have been very understanding. I did not mention this request to the others, of course, until the picture came with the caption: "All good wishes and a long life to the SRSFC, Rex Stout, 6/20/55." This was some months after he had appeared in a group photo at the signing by President Eisenhower of the Universal Copyright Convention; the goatee shows to better advantage in the SRSFC picture!

A postscript to my thank-you letter asking him if Nero Wolfe would mind if we continued to drink cocktails, rather than beer, at SRSFC gatherings, brought the following response (June 20, 1955):

> "A return from a trip is always pleasant, and mine (yes-terday) was made doubly so by your letter describing the inception of SRSFC. It even made me cross the room to a mirror to look at myself.
>
> "NW wouldn't mind at all your drinking cocktails, under one condition. You must not drink whiskey, gin or rum before a dinner with a decent wine. He feels strongly about that. For that matter, so do I!"

The Syracuse Rex Stout Fan Club was unlike any other club I have ever known. It had no constitution or by-laws or dues and only a few secretary's minutes have survived. In addition to the founding members, we soon added Helen Shaffer, Arlene LaRue, Ruth Randell, Lila Piper, Dorothy Rivers and after that many others who evinced an interest in the Stout books.

Members accumulated from chance meetings on downtown street corners, telephone calls, letters, casual acquaintances at parties: when the conversation turned to the magic names of Rex Stout, Nero Wolfe, Archie Goodwin, etc. we had a new member.

In the beginning, a motion was made that our membership "be contained to a very select few with careful screening by the members in good standing to avoid degeneration of our objective which is the mutual appreciation of the writings of Rex Stout." Another motion that men be admitted "was tabled in order that this could have further contemplation by the members." Nothing ever came of that; men were never invited to SRSFC membership. Dinner meetings were bi-monthly, and "when feasible, menus would be in accord with the taste of Mr. Wolfe — unless it is impractical for the hostess."

As it turned out, the SRSFC was, in truth, a meeting of minds. The fun was of exchanging book and ideas, keeping each other informed of anything printed about our author and his characters, and looking for Rex on television. All went well, except when one charter member referred to us as the "The Stout Girls" and it made a newspaper headline that way!

Every once in a while there would be something that I wanted to tell Rex about. For example the time in October, 1956, when I sat next a man by the name of Howard Cullman on an airplane from Washington to New York. He offered me his newspaper which I declined, citing the detective story I was reading. He said that all his most intelligent friends read mysteries and we mentioned our favorite authors. I gave up the idea of reading when he said he knew Rex Stout personally, relating an incident during a convention when he returned to his hotel room and found Rex taking a nap on his bed. Mr. Cullman had something to do with the planning of the United States Exhibit at the Brussels International Fair in 1958 and had just come from a meeting with President Eisenhower. An interesting brush with a stranger through a mutual interest.

My letters to Rex were always lengthy, his replies usually brief but (more than) satisfactory. Sometimes he wasn't as helpful as others, as the reply to my January 26, 1957, letter asking for recipes and other information. He answered it January 28, 1957:

> "It sounds to me as the SRSFC is now about big enough to
> be a pressure group. If so, I hope Katherine Sullivan doesn't
> use a pressure cooker for the dinner on March 22nd. I don't like
> pressure cookers and neither does Fritz or Mr. Wolfe. I'm

enclosing the recipes you wanted and hope that one of them will do.

"I could easily answer the questions that were asked at your dinner meeting Friday evening, but I won't, since once a question is answered it is no longer interesting. Except one: 'Is there a woman who comes in to clean?' Good Lord, no. A man comes in to clean, and some day he is going to . . . but I'll save that for a story I have in mind."

The recipes referred to are on a blue sheet, sixteen of them starting with Mrs. Vail's Baked Beans and ending with Roast Corn-on-the-Cob, Kansas-style, put out by *American Magazine*. This collection of recipes is now one of the most highly coveted items of Stoutiana.

The longest letter I have is dated November 4, 1957, and it came airmail:

"Since getting your letter of September 19th, I have (a) visited my daughter at school at Bennington, (b) eaten a meal with, and made a talk to, the 582 inmates at the Federal Prison at Danbury, c) gone to bed for a week with the flu, (d) watched four World's Series games at Yankee Stadium, (e) chaired two meetings of the Authors League Council, (f) chased twenty-nine deer, including five fawns, from my garden, (g) spent two weeks in the Gulf of Mexico catching kingfish, (h) had a return engagement with the flu, and (I) worried a total of thirty-three hours about Sputnik.

"Might I have managed, somewhere in between, to answer your welcome and delightful letter? Yes. Did I? No.

"I can reply to the four questions you asked. Of course I shall be glad to autograph your *Champagne for One*. No one teaches the parakeets to talk; NW will not permit it. I think George Sanders might make a pretty good Archie, but for ten years I have declined all television and movie offers for NW and AG. The piano in the front room is played only by two people: Fritz Brenner and Saul Panzer. Fritz's repertoire consists of three Chopin preludes, Debussy's *Golliwog's Cakewalk*, "*Marlborough s'en va-t-en Guerre*," and "*Believe Me, If All Those Endearing Young Charms*." Saul plays almost anything, but mostly he improvises.

"I shall be thinking of you Friday evening, and wishing I were there to have a share of your dinner."

One of the early delights of our fan club was finding other Stout stories published before, or in the first days of, the Nero Wolfe series. I especially recall discovering Tecumseh Fox and Dol Bonner and finally, after a long search, a hardcover first edition of *Fer-de-Lance* without a jacket but otherwise in excellent condition. I had fallen into the habit of sending new acquisitions to Rex for his autograph and the inscription in *Fer-de-Lance* is dated February 15, 1958, twenty-four years after its publication date.

The SRSFC took somewhat of a recess for a few years as far as meetings were concerned but continued to add new members whenever they showed proper interest. We remained informal, borrowing and lending the books to share this great store of reading pleasure.

By 1965, my husband had taken an early retirement and our lifestyle began to change. My letter to Rex dated December 1, 1965, reminded him that he was still very much admired by his fan club and asked him about the suggestion in *The Mother Hunt* that Archie might marry Lucy Valdon. I also asked if NW would mind Archie sitting in his chair in his absence. The answer, dated December 4 reads:

"It will be a pleasure to autograph the book, of course. Archie would probably deny it, but I suspect that on those rare occasions that he sits in Wolfe's chair he has a feeling that he is making a concession. As for Wolfe's approval, that concerns him only in professional matters, never in personal ones.

"Marry Lucy Valdon, or anyone, no. It may be that there have been, and are, incidents in his relations with Lucy which he has not mentioned to Lily Rowan, but I am not Paul Pry. In my relations with Archie I avoid giving him an opportunity to tell me to mind my own business."

By the fall of 1966, my husband and I were selling our house in Syracuse, putting our things in storage and taking off for a winter in Florida to find out whether we would like to live there or not.

I wrote to Rex in December, 1966, from Sarasota to wish him a Happy 80th Birthday and to say again, even though the official copy of the brownstone's layout (as shown in *Nero Wolfe of West Thirty-Fifth Street* — Ed.) had duly arrived, that it simply would not work for me, that nothing could disturb my mental image of that house. I underlined the word nothing, but to this day I have never gotten around to considering seriously just where (on the back wall, near Archie's desk?) I like the waterfall picture . . . or the terrestrial globe.

And then there's the question of which side of the street the house is on. Are you for north or south?

My Greetings to Rex Stout on the occasion of his eightieth birthday were acknowledged by this note of December 8, 1966, to our vacation address in Sarasota, Florida:

> "So that's what happened to you: I was wondering. I once caught a 34-lb. kingfish up the coast from Sarasota a few miles. How I love that gulf and the pompano that are sometimes in it!"

Death of a Doxy was out that month, and I remember writing him when I sent him a copy to autograph and I apologized for missing it earlier. My husband and I returned to Syracuse the following spring long enough to make out our income tax return and then went for a three-month trip to Europe.

It was when we were in Rome that Rex Stout's name was mentioned in a chance encounter with an English couple on their way to Sorrento. After dinner one evening, we were sitting in a beautiful walled garden at the back of our hotel in an old part of the city. We mentioned having seen Agatha Christie's long-running play *The Mousetrap* in London.

The talk turned to mystery and detective fiction and without any prompting the husband announced that Rex Stout was one of his favorite American writers. Of course, I had to send Rex a postcard the next day to tell him!

We returned to Sarasota that fall to have a house built, which we moved into the first of February, 1968. *The Writer's Digest* for May of that year had Rex on the cover and inside, an interview conducted by Don Bensen, Editor-in-Chief of Pyramid Books. My letter to Rex of May 28, 1968, started: "What fun it was to read about you in *The Writer's Digest*, then the very next afternoon find *The President Vanishes* in paperback at Charlie's Newsstand on one side of Main Street, cross over and discover in Ellie's Book Store a display of *The Father Hunt*."

I referred to the way he had discussed the reader's suspension of disbelief, and wrote about my own reaction. I continued, "I don't know just what Jacques Barzun means when he calls Archie a 'folk hero' and a lineal descendant of Huck Finn. To me, he is very elegant and polished and man-about-townish. Why do we, as readers, form such definite impressions and keep them so carefully? In any event, I expect NW and Archie to stay as they are, ageless. And Archie to remain his usual suave self. Even when he is drinking a glass of milk at the kitchen table."

I reported hearing from Rex Stout Fan Club members back in Syracuse and meeting people in our new location who also were devotees of his, so it might be that could have a Florida West Coast unit of the West Thirty-Fifth Street Irregulars. His answer, May 31, 1968, reads:

> "And what fun it was to hear from you again. I was, and am, delighted that when you decided for Florida you chose the West Coast. I condemn the East Coast, utterly; but some of my sweetest memories are of duels I have had with fish offshore from Sarasota to Clearwater. One fine March day I . . . but no. I would go on for pages.

"Jacques Barzun and I have discussed Archie Goodwin several times. He is sure he knows more about him than I do."

In a letter to Rex dated March 19, 1969, I commented on a piece in *The Saturday Review* by Patrick Butler, "*The Sidekick Case.*" It appeared on the *Phoenix Nest* page just above an ad for Beam's Choice bourbon advising, "Don't Wolf It Down." I also spoke of *Kings Full of Aces* and inquired about William S. Baring-Gould's *Nero Wolfe of West Thirty-Fifth Street*, asking, since the book was about his work, if it would be proper for him to inscribe it for me. He replied:

> "I never wolfe down bourbon — excuse it please, I mean wolf.
>
> "Since you're going to get William S. Baring-Gould's book, the paragraph about him on the jacket will tell you who he was — he died last year. If you send it to me (and the new omnibus) I shall be delighted to inscribe them to you. I don't think Baring-Gould would object even if he were still around.
>
> "It was nice to hear from you."

That fall *Death of a Dude* came out and I told Rex in a letter of September 22, 1969, that I had to go to a cocktail party to learn about it. I told him that I considered *Nero Wolfe of West Thirty-Fifth Street* a treasure but had not thought of Lily Rowan as a blonde and was surprised that Fritz Brenner had that habit of taking his shoes off that way.

I said the part having the least interest for me was the speculation about where Nero Wolfe came from, who his parents were, where they came from. "For some reason or other, it's quite enough that America's largest detective occupies that oversized chair in the famous premises," I wrote. "How he arrived there, or what his previous life consisted of, is no concern of mine. And while I'm curious about every little detail of the premises, the staff and their current cases — keeping in mind his office remains on the right as you enter from the front door — I'm not a bit interested in this great man's earlier life." I mentioned seeing him on television and liking the photo (showing him opening a bottle of wine in a food preparation setting) in *Time*'s March 21, 1969, issue in connection with the dual reviews of *Nero Wolfe of West Thirty-Fifth Street* and *Kings Full of Aces*. Liked it so much, in fact, that I was tempted to ask for a copy if he could spare one. Rex replied:

> "Good: I'll be expecting your *Death of a Dude*. As for Baring-Gould's remarks about Nero Wolfe's past, they are mostly just guesses, so who cares? Not you or me.
>
> "I decided long ago not to send photographs to anyone until my 90th birthday."

There was an excuse to write him in June, 1970, after I sat across from Anya Kelegian, daughter of Manfred Lee of Ellery Queen fame, at a luncheon. We talked about mystery writers and she said she had met Rex. She was living on Anna Maria Island at the time and was, I believe, a reporter for the *St. Petersburg Times*. On July 1, 1970, he answered:

> "Your letter has me wondering why Manfred Lee's daughter was at a meeting of Pen Women. I'll ask Manny about her next time I see him.
>
> "Thank you for telling me about it."

The signature on this letter was not as strong as usual, and I wondered if he had been ill. By the time he wrote again, though, it was back to normal.

Meanwhile, it had been discovered that my husband had terminal cancer. He died in August, 1971, and when I wrote Rex about it a year later I also mentioned I heard him being paged in the Atlanta airport as I was flying North that summer. His answer, written on December 11, 1972:

> "No, you don't need to tell me how difficult it has been, and how

different life is, without your husband. And all you can get, like Bert Williams in the song he made famous many years ago, is sympathy.

"No, I wasn't in Atlanta last August; I was here, glad to be outdoors most of the time, doing garden chores."

After returning from a trip to Mexico City, I wrote on October 30, 1973, that I was sending my copy of *Please Pass the Guilt* for the usual treatment. Also, that I had been pleased to see an extensive display of his books in the Mizrachi Bookshop across from the Palacio de Belles Artes in Mexico City.

One of the charter members of the SRSFC, Frannie Tucker, sent me a newspaper clipping of Beth Merriman's October 28, 1973 column in *Parade Magazine* featuring Nero Wolfe's way with a walnut pudding. It showed Rex holding the finished product. One of my bridge partners, neither a cook nor, I am sorry to say, a detective story buff, told me she had a difficult time finding the Marsala wine called for in the recipe when she attempted to make it for Thanksgiving dinner.

Rex provided a flurry of excitement for his fans during the fall of 1973 with two books, *Please Pass the Guilt* and *The Nero Wolfe Cookbook*, and various personal appearances. I was unable to see it, but the first airing of his television appearance with Bob Cromie on *Book Beat* also took place during this time. A friend taped it for me, and others reported on it with enthusiasm.

When I thanked Rex for inscribing these two books dated November 3, 1973, with "warm regards;" the cookbook undated this time but with "best wishes" in green ink, I went on and on, as usual. I don't think he minded and I never minded that his answers were brief.

In this case, I told him I had forgotten Wolfe liked words such as amphigoric and subreption, and that for the first time (in *Please Pass the Guilt*), we found him wearing a yellow smock in the potting room. I asked if this was something new for him or had he always worn a yellow smock while working with his orchids. I have to report he never answered this question. Neither did he comment when I told him a Florida friend, to whom I had loaned *Fer-de-Lance* (so she could start at the beginning) had referred to him as "That adorable Rex Stout." I don't think he cared for that very much. Having a personal liking for pro football, I must have asked him how members of the Wolfe household felt about sports because in his answer of December 7, 1973, he says:

> "What a nice newsy letter, and of course for me good tidings since it was about me. Yes, send the cookbook.
> "NW likes neither football nor baseball. AG likes baseball but not football."

That was to be my last personal note from Rex Stout. The printed "To Whom It May Concern" of December 27, 1973, was included with a letter from Prof. John J. McAleer in February 1974, when he advised me that Rex had authorized him to write his biography which would be published by Little, Brown & Co.

In June of that year, I finally saw the *Book Beat* interview on television as a repeat. When I wrote Rex to tell him how much I enjoyed it, I sent excerpts of letters I had received from other fans as a result of gathering information that might be useful for the biography.

In my copy of the UPI article from a Syracuse newspaper of October 27, 1974, announcing "Author Rex Stout Warming Up to Write A New Nero Wolfe," Rex is quoted as saying, "I never write in the summer; I'll start one on November 19th at 4 o'clock. I'll probably be finished the middle of January. Come out the middle of June, something like that, if I'm alive. I could die; good God, I'm 87 years old. In fact, if I didn't want more than my share, I'd have died quite a while ago." The accompanying photo showed him holding his cigar at an angle, laughing, the goatee now a full white beard.

John McAleer had been keeping me advised of his failing health and says the last book was actually started November 6, 1974, and finished on January 6, 1975.

I purchased two copies of *A Family Affair*, one for myself and the other for the first secretary of our SRSFC and had them mailed to Rex from the store September 3, 1975. They were not returned as promptly as usual. John informed me Rex had been gravely ill, hospitalized, and still a bed patient at home. He wrote me afterward that he had spoken to Rex's daughter Rebecca, who asked Rex if he would like to sign the books and he said he would. I found them in my mailbox the day after his death was announced. They provided a kind of consolation as I carried them into the house.

The Black Mountain, because it was the first book for the auction, *Fer-de-Lance*, because it was autographed so many years after it was written and *A Family Affair*, its inscription undated, the "warm regards" and signature not very firm, have to be my three most treasured of all the Stout volumes.

Certain questions remain. I have often wondered if there is anyone anywhere who has read the Nero Wolfe stories in chronological order. And, if it's more fun that way. (Seriously, I would like to find out if there is such a person.)

As for me, isn't it great that I had not? Otherwise, I could never have written that postscript to my first letter questioning the ground plan of the brownstone. And think of all the fun I would have missed!

REX STOUT — MINISTER OF PROPAGANDA

by Charles E. Burns

IN JOHN MCALEER'S excellent biography of Rex Stout, he devotes eight chapters to Stout as "Minister of Propaganda." And this comprehensive emphasis on Stout's contributions before and during the years of World War II is more than justified. For, as he was a genius in creating Nero Wolfe mysteries, he was equally talented in combatting the flow of Axis lies that spewed forth even before Pearl Harbor. When he foresaw the inevitability of United States' involvement in the war, he pulled no punches, even welcoming the title of "warmonger."

As Chairman of the War Writers Board, Stout mobilized nearly 5,000 writers in the service of the United States war effort. In the first year alone, the Board commissioned and placed over 8,000 stories, articles, radio scripts, and speeches. One of the most successful efforts was a series of sixty-two weekly network radio broadcasts titled *Our Secret Weapon*. It used a dialogue format with actors playing the part of Axis commentators and Stout, the lie detective, offering his refutations.

I was recently reminded of this series when I came across a book titled *To Hasten the Homecoming: How Americans Fought World War II Through the Media* by Jordan Braverman. He cites some of the rumors spread by the Axis through short-wave radio: "The British didn't have rationing like the United States and were joyriding throughout England on American tires and gasoline. The Red Cross didn't really need human blood because animal blood was just as effective. America promised to feed Russia and England even if its own babies had to starve. President Roosevelt and the U. S. Treasury Department had no intention of ever redeeming war bonds and stamps. There were 12,000 British agents in the United States and some of them were sabotaging factories to create fifth-column hysteria."

As ridiculous as these stories may sound in retrospect, remember that we didn't have the instant news and communications of today. Braverman cites one example of *Our Secret Weapon*:

In August 1942 The Columbia Broadcasting System (CBS) began to air a program called *Our Secret Weapon*. Rex Stout, the author and creator of Nero Wolfe, the fictional detective, hosted the program.

According to *Newsweek*, each week Stout would review some 30,000 short-waved Axis words, select pertinent lies, dig up the truth, and write an exposing script. A typical exchange would be

> **ANNOUNCER (German accent):** *The best soldiers and officers in the United States Army are Germans. So are the best baseball and football players.*

> **STOUT (with sarcasm):** *As you can see, they've got the facts, no getting away from it. Take the six leading batters in the major leagues: Williams. Gordon. Wright. Reiser. Lombardi. Medwich. Some bunch of Germans. Also, the great German prize fighter, Joe Louis.*

The show was such a success that orders for scripts were running as high as 6,000 a week. When Stout heard that the show was beginning to annoy the German Ministry of Propaganda, he answered on another program:

> Great heavens. I hope these little broadcasts I do aren't bothering Dr. Goebbels. I am a man of good will. I wish him the best. I hope he is boiled in the very best oil — none of that ersatz stuff.

Braverman added that "Sometimes the program dramatized German, Italian, and Japanese speeches, with actors playing the roles of Hitler, Mussolini, and Hirohito."

As Wolfe would conclude: Satisfactory.

POLA WEINBERG STOUT (1902-1984)

by Eleanor Sullivan

WHEN REX STOUT died in October 1975, I wrote a note of sympathy to his wife Pola. I had never met her or Rex face to face and had only spoken on the telephone with Rex twice, very briefly, in connection with Nero Wolfe stories we were reprinting in *Ellery Queen's Mystery Magazine,* but I was a great admirer and told Pola so. In July of the following year I received a phone call at the office from her about my note and what it had meant to her. After we said goodbye, I sat for minutes, struck dumb by the depth of the emotion she had articulated — the rareness of it and the intelligence of it.

Our friendship began that day and while it was manifested mostly in phone calls (over a hundred of them), we did meet at four social occasions: Carol Brener's Rex Stout Dinner at the Lotos Club in November 1977; the supper sponsored by Davis Publications after the showing of *The Doorbell Rang* at the Second International Congress of Crime Writers at The Biltmore in March 1978; the first Wolfe Pack Dinner at the Gramercy Park Hotel in December of the same year; and the second Wolfe Pack Dinner at The Biltmore the following December. And I enjoyed two wonderful weekends with her at High Meadow, in September 1978 and May 1979, and visited her once at the Courtlandt Gardens in Stamford in 1981.

She was always hopeful, always "getting better," by which she meant as energetic and functioning as she had been in the years before Rex's long illness and death before I knew her. But the Pola I knew functioned with as much energy and purpose as most adults. A young man from the Prisco Cab Company who drove me to the Brewster train station after my first weekend visit was so mesmerized by her warmth and charm he could hardly bring himself to start up the car and leave — a reluctance he admitted during the drive to the station. Somehow she had made us feel wonderful about ourselves and the world we lived in.

Pola designed for Botany Mills and in 1946, underwritten by eight manufacturers, she set up her own textile mill in North Philadelphia. She created fabrics for Dior, Mainbocher, Norell, Trigere, Irene, Adrian, and many other major designers. She taught and conducted seminars all over the country, including at Harvard University. Exhibits of her textiles were held at the Philadelphia Museum College of Art and, in New York, at the Museum of Contemporary Crafts and (for a full year) at the Fashion Institute of Technology.

In a talk she gave in September 1958 in conjunction with her exhibition "Fabrics by Pola Stout" at the Philadelphia Museum she said:

> "One of my abiding convictions as a designer has been that women must have clothes they can depend on, clothes to give them dignity and poise. There is an intangible quality that exists when clothes look as if they belong to their owners, when they are appropriate for the occasion and are being worn with confidence and enjoyment. That's why I have stressed the theme that the costume of a new season should always be planned to harmonize with your best choices of past seasons, so that wardrobes can be built from year to year.
>
> "Yes, I know most of us love new things, we want to follow fashion; but do we want the coat we buy today to start a violent quarrel with other wearable dresses and skirts in our closets? Wardrobes — and, for that matter, interiors — should be

planned so that, having selected a basically suitable range of fabrics and color, our subsequent choices make added sense and beauty within the selected framework . . . just as the social unit is not the husband, the wife, or the child, but the family, so the wardrobe unit should not be the skirt, dress, suit, or coat, but the ensemble."

The phone rang often at High Meadow — with calls from Rex and Pola's daughters Barbara and Rebecca and from Pola's many friends, including Marian Anderson. Although the walls were hung with many photographs of family and friends and the rooms were full of fine art and love tokens and objects that bespoke a busy, well-run household, they were still remarkably uncluttered, the lines clean, and great open spaces always ready for work or some large gesture of hospitality.

Because her energy was fragile, she had to pace herself, and yet it seemed to me that Pola moved almost always at a graceful run. She prepared delicious, nourishing meals in the modest kitchen with no apparent effort while carrying on lively conversation. The kitchen was surprisingly small — utilitarian without flash. We sat at the table there for hours before and after meals, Czarna, the Stouts' noble black Labrador resting silently nearby, constantly, adoringly attuned to Pola.

What did we talk about? Rex, of course, and the exciting, exacting differences between the sexes. About politics, education, food, my work and hers. For example, after the Givenchy retrospective at the Fashion Institute several years ago I told Pola on the phone that I'd always found his clothes remote, and she explained that he had always been financially independent, which gave him the freedom to experiment and express himself in a less down-to-earth way than a more restricted designer would.

Shortly after we first met, I asked her when she had become interested in fashion and she told me that as a little girl in Poland she had dressed and redressed her three dolls every day, in clothes she made for them, and displayed them in a window facing the street.

Changing the clothes every day was an important effort to brighten the days for those who passed by.

She was occupied with an extraordinary, painstaking project — the design of fifty plaids, one for each of the United States — a tangible appreciation of the adopted country she loved and felt deeply indebted to. The twenty or so I saw finished or partially completed were exquisite.

She spoke several times about another project she had in mind, one she wanted my help with when it was time: a Rex Stout scholarship program for public-school children. (What could be a more appropriate memorial for the co-founder of the Educational Thrift Service?) The evening she first spoke of it I was coming down with one of the Great Colds of My Life, which she dosed with whiskey and lemon. I slept in different guest rooms my two visits to High Meadow and both were furnished with every comfort a guest could want, including books galore and Kleenex galore — so the sleeplessness induced by the early stages of a bad cold were well served by literature, a full box of tissues, and the effects of Pola's hot toddies and catalytic conversation. I drifted in and out of sleep, speculating on her scholarship idea and how there probably would need to be a juvenile biography of Rex attendant to the plan and that a good working title for it might be *Boy of the Frontier, Man of the World*.

AT THE end of each of my visits to High Meadow, Pola sent me back to New York with a massive bouquet of flowers from the garden and on the second visit she gave me a wool-tweed pullover she had designed and woven herself in lovely shades of brown, black, and white. On both visits, too, she gave me fruit and vegetables to bring home — gathered by Harold Salmon, son of Adelbert Salmon, who owned the farmhouse at the foot of the hill that Rex had rented before he built High Meadow. Harold, who Pola relied on for a great many things, as she and Rex had for years, drove me to the train after my second visit, and looking back on our conversation I can see that he was already grieving for a Pola he had known that I hadn't.

But the Pola I knew was a rare and beautiful creature. Her exceptional emotional makeup, her mischievous (not childish) sense of humor, her original and honest way of expressing herself were truly unique. Her greeting to me was always the same and will serve to express how I will always feel about her:

Dearest woman.

REX STOUT, NERO WOLFE, AND LAWRENCE OF ARABIA

by Robert Franks

IN (W. S.) BARING-GOULD'S *Nero Wolfe of West 35th Street*, Rex Stout mentions two books he would liked to have written:

> The last dozen books I've seen which deal with literature in the English language in the last century almost never mention the book that I would rather have written than any other one book in the language . . . *Alice in Wonderland*. A close second is T. E. Lawrence's *Seven Pillars of Wisdom*. While Alice is universally recognized, *Seven Pillars of Wisdom* is little known today, though it was considered a masterpiece in the 1930's.

Most people know that T. E. Lawrence was "Lawrence of Arabia," the English guerrilla leader who led the Arabs in their revolt against the Turks during World War I. But few people know that after the war, Lawrence wrote a six-hundred-page epic about his part in the revolt, calling it *Seven Pillars of Wisdom*. This book, part military history and part autobiography, was the basis of David Lean's Academy Award-winning 1962 film, "Lawrence of Arabia," starring Peter O'Toole and Omar Sharif.

Lawrence felt that he had betrayed the Arabs by promising them self-rule, a promise which he knew his government could not fulfill. Ashamed of his role in the revolt, he refused to profit by it in any way. Therefore when he finished his book in 1926, he privately published a limited "subscriber's edition" of 216 copies at thirty guineas each (about $90). He did not receive a shilling from his enterprise.

John McAleer writes that in 1928 Rex Stout "read a subscriber's copy of T. E. Lawrence's *Seven Pillars of Wisdom* and reread it twice more. 'It belongs on the shelf of the very best.'" Time would erode that view somewhat but, at 88, Rex still thought it a "wonderful writing job."

Though Stout never corresponded directly nor met Lawrence in person, the latter did have a chance to read one of Stout's early novels.

In 1931, Rex's non-Nero novel, *Seed on the Wind*, was published in England by Mitchell Kennerly. Christopher Morley was so impressed by that book that he asked his brother, who knew Kennerly, to request that copies be sent to H. G. Wells, Herbert Read, and T. E. Lawrence.

Unfortunately there is no evidence that Lawrence read the book. But *Seed on the Wind* was reviewed by the novelist and critic Richard Aldington. Aldington disliked Stout's book: "This book is the homunculus in the bottle, the synthetic product without the vitally necessary vitamins, a full-sized oak in papier-mâché.'

Ironically, Aldington was later to treat Stout's idol even more harshly. In 1955, Aldington wrote an iconoclastic and vitriolic attack on Lawrence, called *Lawrence of Arabia: A Biographical Enquiry*. Admirers of Lawrence are still reeling from this vicious jeremiad against their hero.

While Rex Stout was reading *Seven Pillars of Wisdom* in 1926, its enigmatic author was retreating from the limelight. He enlisted as a lowly private in the Royal Air Force. Lawrence's rejection of fame and fortune at the height of his popularity dismayed his devotees, yet at the same time his enlistment increased interest in his book. He was dubbed "the mystery man of Europe and Asia."

But the more Lawrence hid, the more reporters sought him out. He even legally changed his name to T. E. Shaw in an attempt to escape from the public scrutiny.

Lawrence died at age 47 from injuries sustained in a motor-cycle accident. There was some question of a cover-up regarding Lawrence's death. A mysterious black car was spotted near the scene of the crash. Unsubstantiated rumors circulated which claimed that the fledgling Nazi party, which feared that Lawrence might re-emerge as a viable leader, staged the "accident."

Was Lawrence of Arabia murdered?

It would have been marvelous if Rex Stout himself had investigated Lawrence's untimely death. But unlike Conan Doyle, Stout did not involve himself in real-life murders. Fortunately, he did the next best thing: he wrote about Lawrence in one of his Nero Wolfe mysteries.

In many of the novels, Archie mentions Wolfe's "current book." Archie spends much of his time urging Wolfe to pursue the mystery at hand instead of burying himself in a book.

These "current books" are of course ones that Rex Stout himself had read and enjoyed. Because he was fascinated by Lawrence and *Seven Pillars*, Stout chose to publicize it in *The Red Box*, published a year after Lawrence's death.

Archie writes:

> Wolfe was at his desk with a book, *Seven Pillars of Wisdom* by Lawrence, which he had already read twice, and I knew that mood he was in when I saw that the tray and glass were on his desk but no empty bottle . . . I tossed my notebook on the desk and sat down and sipped the milk. There was no use trying to explode him off that book. But after a while he picked up the thin strip of ebony he used for a bookmark, inserted it, closed the book, laid it down, and reached out and rang for beer.

But Archie has not heard the last of *Seven Pillars of Wisdom*. As they dine, Wolfe treats his assistant to an analysis of Lawrence's success with the Arabs. Archie writes:

> He read until dinner time, but even *Seven Pillars of Wisdom* did not restrain his promptness in responding to Fritz's sum-

mons to table. During the meal he kindly explained to me the chief reason for Lawrence's amazing success in keeping the Arabian tribes together for the great revolt. It was because Lawrence's personal attitude toward women was the same as the classic and traditional Arabian attitude. The central fact about any man, in respect to his activities as a social animal, is his attitude toward women: hence the Arabs felt that essentially Lawrence was one of them, and so accepted him. His native ability for leadership and finesse did the rest. A romantic they would not have understood, a puritan they would have rudely ignored, a sentimentalist they would have laughed at, but the contemptuous realist Lawrence, with his false humility and his fierce secret pride, they took to their bosoms.

Archie was indifferent to the reasons that Lawrence was successful. Nero Wolfe, however, was persistent. We learn twelve pages later that "He resumed with the atlas, doing the double page spread of Arabia." Obviously the location of the red box would have to wait until Wolfe had satisfied his curiosity about a geographical point in *Seven Pillars*. A page later Wolfe is still immersed in his atlas: "Wolfe stayed in Arabia. I cleared my throat like a lion and his eyes flickered at me."

Undoubtedly Wolfe's curiosity, much to Archie's mounting frustration, was still focused upon the sandy wastes of Arabia. Archie does not say in *The Red Box* if Wolfe was reading the "subscriber's" edition or a less expensive trade edition published later under the title *Revolt in the Desert*. But (since) Wolfe demanded only the best of everything, from orchids and *saucisse minuit* to the best books and dining at Rusterman's, it is reasonable to assume that, like his creator, he was regarding the magnificent "subscriber's" edition.

Perhaps he even sacrificed the purchase of some Cymbidium in order to pay for the expensive tome.

What is it about Lawrence's book that so fascinated Wolfe? Two major factors are Wolfe's passionate love of language and his equally passionate aversion to women.

Wolfe is a renowned logophile. Archie often wonders which

Wolfe loves more, food or words. In the saga, we come across such rare words as "apodictial," "gibbosit," "rodomontade" and "usufructs." In *T. E. Lawrence by His Friends* (1937), Robert Graves relates how Lawrence used recondite words:

> Professor Edgeworth, of All Souls (Oxford) avoided conversational English, confidently using words and phrases that one only expected to meet in books. One day Lawrence was returning from a visit to London and Edgeworth met him at the gate.
>
> "Was it very caliginous in the Metropolis?"
>
> "Somewhat caliginous, but not altogether inspissated," Lawrence replied gravely.

Nero Wolfe was an admirer of not only words, but of the artistic arrangements of words. Here is an excerpt from the epilogue to *Seven Pillars*, which demonstrates Lawrence's prose:

> Damascus had not seemed a sheath for my sword, when I landed in Arabia: but its capture disclosed the exhaustion of my main springs of action. The strongest motive throughout had been a personal one, not mentioned here, but present to me, I think, every hour of these two years. Active pains and joys might fling up, like towers, among my days: but refluent as air, this hidden urge re-formed, to be the persisting element of life, till near the end. It was dead, before we reached Damascus . . . I had dreamed, at the City School in Oxford, of hustling into form, while I lived, the new Asia which time was inexorably bringing upon us . . . Fantasies, these will seem, to such as are able to call my beginning an ordinary effort.

I can hear Wolfe murmuring, "Satisfactory."

But the mastery of words evident in *Seven Pillars* was only one of the reasons Wolfe venerated the book. Lawrence's attitude toward women mirrored not only the Arabs' view, but also Wolfe's. The detective found in Lawrence a kindred soul whose virulent dislike of women matched his own.

Lawrence's misogyny was well known. He wrote,

Women? I like some women. I don't like their sex: any more than I like the monstrous regiment of men. There is no difference that I feel between a woman and a man.

In another of his letters, Lawrence expressed himself slightly differently . . .

Please believe that I don't either love or hate the entire sex of woman. There are good ones and bad ones, I find, much the same as men and dogs and motor bicycles.

Lawrence also excluded women from Parnassus. "All the women who ever wrote original stuff could have been strangled at birth, and the history of English (and my bookshelves) would be unchanged."

Lawrence's life in the RAF insulated him from the opposite sex. "Being a mechanic cuts one off from all real communication with women," Lawrence explained. In Wolfe's case, the old brownstone was his haven against females. However, sometimes a woman would cross his threshold and actually talk to him. If she broke down under his questioning and starting crying, Wolfe would invariably flee the room, leaving Archie to console the distraught woman.

Wolfe outlines his position regarding women in *Too Many Cooks* (1938).

Not like women? They are astonishing and successful animals. For reasons of convenience, I merely preserve an appearance of immunity which I developed some years ago under the pressure of necessity.

It is not clear what his "necessity" was. An unhappy marriage, perhaps? Or did Wolfe fear that a woman would interfere with his intellectual pursuits?

Yet Wolfe is contradictory. He also says:

Not that I disapprove of women, except when they attempt to function as domestic animals. When they stick to the vocations for which they are best adapted, such as chicanery, sophistry, self-advertisement, cajolery, mystification, and incubation, they are sometimes superb creatures.

In *The Silent Speaker* (1946), Archie attempts to analyze Wolfe's phobia: "I had made a close and prolonged study of Wolfe's attitude toward women. The basic fact about women that seemed to irritate him was that she was a woman: the long record showed not a single exception, but from there on the documentation was cockeyed. If woman as woman grated on him you would suppose that the most womanly details would be the worst for him, but time and again I have known him to have a chair placed for the female so that his desk would not obstruct his view of her legs . . . It is a very complex question and someday I'm going to take a whole chapter for it. Another little detail: he is much more sensitive to women's noses than he is to men's . . . "

Although Archie did not write this proposed chapter, we can conclude that Wolfe basically viewed women as illogical, intimidating beings. Yet his attitude was not entirely chauvinistic. Wolfe, as Archie tells us, was not above admiring a woman's leg. As for Lawrence, he was distressed by the physical attributes of women but he formed one of the most intimate relationships of his life with a female. This woman, however, was Charlotte Shaw, the playwright's wife. Being well over sixty, she was deemed safe by Lawrence.

We can see that Wolfe's veneration of *Seven Pillars of Wisdom* had its roots in both his love of language and his views of women which were endorsed by Lawrence. To Wolfe, the chief reason for Lawrence's success was that his anti-women attitude was approved of by the Arabs. Wolfe, however, has been blinded by his own prejudices. It took more than misogyny to unite the fractious tribes into a guerilla force capable of defeating a vastly superior enemy. Equally important to Lawrence's spectacular success was his ability to see into men's souls, his complete immersion of the Arab way of life and his unswerving belief that the Arabs were capable of governing themselves. Because his is an immortal character, Nero Wolfe never ages. The great detective will have ample time in which to ease his seventh of a ton into his favorite chair and reread *Seven Pillars of Wisdom*, enjoying the memorable prose and relishing the thought that Lawrence, like himself, was a genius and a misogynist of the first order. Hopefully, in one of Robert Goldsborough's new pastiches, we will read that "Wolfe was at his desk with a book he had already read six times, *Seven Pillars of Wisdom* by Lawrence."

RECIPE FOR A COOKBOOK

by Barbara Burn

LIKE ONE of Fritz Brenner's sauces, creation of *The Nero Wolfe Cookbook* required loving attention and long, slow preparation. It also involved lighting a fire under Rex Stout, who was unenthusiastic about the project at first. Fans had requested such a book for years, but Stout always dismissed the idea as "too much work." Finally Helen Taylor, then in charge of cookbooks at The Viking Press, convinced Stout that Viking editors would work out all the recipes and that all he need do would be to give his approval.

After Stout reluctantly agreed, Helen and I spent many delightful hours rereading the books and listing every food reference. Since Viking's office had neither a test kitchen nor a Fritz Brenner, our efforts were limited to extracting our favorite culinary quotes and hoping that somehow the recipes would emerge by wishful thinking. Eventually the project was pushed to the back burner where it simmered away quietly, never going cold but definitely not making it to the table.

In 1973, when I became an editor at Viking, I inherited the task of looking after the cookbook projects. At about the same time I moved into an apartment which actually had a kitchen with four walls and a stove with four burners.

One evening I found myself hungry for corn fritters. I tried a couple of recipes but the results weren't very satisfying. It wasn't until several experiments later, following a conversation with a

Southern friend, that I arrived at a concoction that worked. I was a few pounds heavier than on the day I moved into my new apartment, but I had also gained an inspiration. Aha, I thought. I'll do the recipes myself and we'll get a Nero Wolfe cookbook at last.

Twenty pounds and several hundred dollars later, most of them devoted to shad roe, peanut-fed pigs, and the like, I gave up. I had completed about thirty recipes, but had over a hundred to go, not counting the ones that Stout and Sheila Hibben, the late *New Yorker* writer, had devised for a special edition of *Too Many Cooks*. Luckily, one of Viking's salesmen in those days, Mike Romano, doubled as a caterer and chef. Mike joined my search for the best ways to turn my notes into a cookbook. Sometimes our only clue was the title of an exotic dish, sometimes it was a list of ingredients, sometimes only one. Mike's worst problem was pesto for which, along with two cups of basil, Wolfe insisted on a quarter pound of pig's liver. (Upon hearing this in "The Zero Clue," Lt. Cramer reacted with a heartfelt "Good God!") Mike's Italian family had practically weaned him on pesto, but he had never heard pig's liver mentioned in the same breath as basil, let alone in the same dish. Then one day, on a selling trip in upper New York State, Mike stopped at a restaurant in the town of Deposit, where the chef offered some help. "I've never heard of that particular combination," he told Mike, "but let's try." After a two hour session in the kitchen, the two of them triumphantly produced a pesto that was not only edible but delicious. At last the cookbook was ready for writing.

My task was somewhat complicated by the idiosyncratic tastes of the household on West 35th Street. I had to accommodate Archie's corned beef as well as Wolfe's *sauce Vatel*. And what was I to do with a culinary genius who spawned four recipes for shad roe but only one for flounder? Half a lamb cooked twenty different ways but no roast beef? Six corn recipes but none for peas? Obviously, this book would not be the usual fish, meat and vegetable manual.

I took off a week from work and typed for six days straight, stopping only for milk and beer, which somehow made the work go faster. I lost twenty pounds and gained a 300-page manuscript that I proudly bore back to Viking.

Then a chilling idea struck: what if Stout hated it? What if all that work had been in vain? I didn't have to hold my breath long. Within a week after I mailed his copy, Stout called and asked me to come see him. When I arrived he told me that he had read about one-sixth of the recipes and thought they were fine. He then asked if I'd like Fritz to write a foreword, and if it would be okay to include a recipe for frog's legs, which had somehow never made it into any of the stories. I agreed at once. One of the few criticisms was that I liked parsley and onions too much. "I grow shallots by the bushel up here," Stout explained. "They are much better than onions and people really mince them because they're so small."

After making a mental note to substitute shallots for every onion in the manuscript, I screwed up my courage to ask Stout a few questions. "What kind of stove does Fritz have?" I said, thinking the answer would be, "Gas." Stout surprised me. "A big electric range," he replied, "and an anthracite-burning stove which is warm enough on the back to keep a stock pot going and salt-rising bread rising." Undaunted, I wondered, like Archie, about all the shad roe. Why hadn't fish figured out some other way? Whales had. After some thought Stout told me that those stories must have been written in New York City in May, when shad roe was in season and very much on his mind. "I wish there were more flounder recipes," he added. "Flounder is the greatest fish in the East. Growing up in Kansas I never had fish, but when I came East I remember that flounder. Better than Dover sole."

The afternoon evaporated and all too soon it was time to leave. Three days later I received a recipe for frog's legs, a foreword by Fritz, and a promise of Stout's new novel, for which I was to be his editor. The cookbook was published within the year and is now in its seventh printing. My greatest reward, however, was the chance once again to read the stories for themselves and not as a source for recipes. Still, I must admit that even now I automatically reach for a pencil every time Wolfe and Archie walk into the dining room on West 35th Street.

A LABOR OF LOVE:
THE NERO WOLFE
TELEVISION SERIES

by Michael Jaffe

(*Mr. Jaffe, executive producer of A&E's Nero Wolfe series, was keynote speaker at the 2001 Black Orchid Banquet.*)

I'M DELIGHTED to be here. I usually don't accept invitations of this type but my involvement with Nero Wolfe goes back a long time, to the early '70s, and I've been aware of your group for some time. Earlier someone asked if this has had an impact on the series and how it could have an impact on A&E. I responded with a simple statistic. I also produce A&E's *100 Center Street*. On the A&E website, *100 Center Street* received 1,200 hits. Nero Wolfe received more than 13,800, which for me is not actually a surprise. I always believed from the beginning that Nero Wolfe, particularly on the A&E channel which is geared to people who think, would be a successful series. But I only believed it would be a successful series if A&E let us produce the series the way the series was meant to be produced.

As you all know, there once was a series produced by Paramount. Let me tell you about my first introduction to a possible Nero Wolfe series. Larry Marks, who was a senior vice president of film for Warner Brothers Studios in the early '70s, and my father, who was actively producing for television, had come to New York to meet with Rex Stout's agent. He had decided to market the rights and Larry Marks was a good friend of my father's. At any rate, Warner Brothers was very interested in making a feature film and their plan, according to Larry Marks, was to take all of the Zeck stories and end, of course, with *In the Best Families.* Their big question was how to make him fat and how to make him thin using the same actor. The idea was to get George C. Scott and pad him. In any event, Larry Marks called my father and he asked me to read the books. I did and I loved them. I worked very hard trying to get the rights. As you all can surmise, I didn't, Paramount did. You saw what they did to it. I don't mean to trash things and I think it's indicative of the '80s, but the Paramount series made every single bad choice that could be made. Bad cast. Awful art direction. Wardrobe was appalling. The period they chose was dreadful. The sets were unspeakably bad. But worst of all they didn't respect the Canon. They didn't respect the work. They thought the most important thing about a Nero Wolfe story was the stories or the plots. They thought they could rip off stories here and there and that any old normal series dialogue would work. Well, obviously they missed the point.

This is where an Orson Welles story comes in. Those of you who are sensitive to foul language, raise your hand. (*laughter*) No one? Good. Orson was a devoted reader and had probably read all the Nero Wolfe books. He understood the material as well as anyone and, just on the surface of it, Welles was the perfect Nero Wolfe. It's all downhill from here. A producer — who will remain nameless — was in charge of writing the Paramount show. He called Orson in to interview him for the role of Nero Wolfe. Orson Welles was a brilliant, extraordinary presence, he had a chameleon presence and the quickest wit in the world. The only reason he went to this meeting was in the tiny hope that maybe Paramount would do it right. Welles walked into the meeting and the producer said "Now, Orson." The producer lost him right there. Orson Welles was a very formal guy. He had never met this man and didn't feel this man had the right to address him as "Orson." The producer continued, "Now, Orson. I've been thinking about this and what we have to do is make Nero Wolfe more human." If you remember the series that's what they did. They made him a sweetie pie, saccharine. It was awful. "We have to make him someone more accessible to the American public . . . " the producer said. And without missing a beat, Orson Welles turned to the producer and said, "Making Nero Wolfe human is a little bit like asking Don Juan to have a soft prick." He didn't say good-bye. He just left. Orson was not somebody to fool around with. He was a tough guy.

We finally got this opportunity. I've been friends with the estate since the early '70s and I had chased the rights numerous times. One of the reasons that I never actually tried to make it as a series was that I didn't believe a network would ever let us make it the right way. Then A&E came along and Alan Sabinson. I've known him for years and years. He swore he'd let me make it the right way. That was *Golden Spiders*. What we had really envisioned was a series of two-hour movies, maybe one and a half a year. But *Golden Spiders* was the highest rating that A&E got for a two-hour movie. This astounded them. I was not surprised and I'm on record as having said I'm not. It's not hindsight.

Alan then came to Tim (Hutton) and me and said, "Would you be willing to make a series?" So Tim and I went away and huddled and then back to Alan after some days and we had a meeting. Basically we said to Alan that we would only be willing to do a series if you respect the material, you don't tell us how to write it or tell us how to cast it. And, you agree right now that for the first time in the history of any television series — and this is one of the truly unique things in the Nero Wolfe Series — that episodes would be based entirely on author-written material.

All other series are based on a concept, but the writers create the stories and material. I felt that was impossible. A&E said then we're sort of limited and I responded that you have seventy-two stories and thirty-odd are long, so we can easily make two-hour stories. So we could conceivably get to 100 hours, and if we get there the people will be so old that we can start over again!

Eventually A&E agreed to do the show the way we wanted to do it. Now let's talk about that vision for a minute. Tim has a lot of very specific ideas and notions about how to do this. What I enjoy about Nero Wolfe is not the plots, and if this is heresy so be it. I don't care about the stories. The plots are just vehicles and they're vehicles for what we called "obligatory scenes." Fabulous obligatory scenes where you knew, you could predict, what was going to happen in the dialogue between a great set of characters. My best example of this to people who are not familiar with Nero Wolfe material is the old Colombo series. Remember, there was always that moment in the show when Peter Falk would say to someone, "I don't have any more questions" and then he'd snap his fingers and "You know, I do have one more question." I'm convinced that people tuned that show in for that moment. That's why they watched that series. I think in my case, at least I hoped, that people watched the Nero Wolfe series to see those moments that they expect to see having read the books. Those are the interchanges with Archie and Nero Wolfe and, if it were up to Sharon (Doyle, Head Writer), it would be nothing but Wolfe and Fritz in the kitchen and Cramer carrying on. That's what we grow to expect.

We've filmed our series around the notion that those moments are critical, and if we choose between trying to explicate the plot for a television audience or giving them a cool bit of dialogue between Stebbins and Archie, we will always use the dialogue. And if that means the audience can't follow the plot, then we'll cut that piece of the plot out.

I was talking to about five or six people before about the stories and really at the end of the day when you dissect the plots they're just crazy. As an example of that, we're doing *The Silent Speaker* in March and you'll all remember the John Smith scene when the guy comes and says, "I'll give you a billion dollars to fabricate the evidence." It became clear that I couldn't explain to a television audience in the ninety minutes that we have where he was coming from and why he was there. It threw the story off. And, the interesting thing in the novel is, and you will see this is the case, take the John Smith scene out and you don't miss it. Well, you miss it because you knew it was there, you read it, and it was great fun when you read it. But in the context of a two-hour film where we have limited time, you don't miss this scene. The hardest thing that we have to do when we adapt these things is to truncate the dialogue. I have adapted two scripts now and my biggest problem is that I'd like to see all the speeches go on forever. Maury (Chaykin), who can't remember his lines, excuse me, I didn't say that, doesn't. Well, he does yell a lot. I've heard that complaint. He did give me a personal message to pass on to anyone who objects to his roaring. I know that there are a lot of people who do, including Sharon and me, although I didn't say that. Maury says, "If you're going to object, I'm going to yell more, I promise you."

For me this has been a labor of love. We have done our best to be loyal to the spirit of the novels, and I have actually enjoyed some of the emails on the A&E website. I've posted three or four answers to people's queries. One of the things that really interested me and I don't say this in fun although it is kind of fun for me, there are a lot of objections that Nero Wolfe didn't have a yellow shirt on. We had some wardrobe problems and we've gotten that straightened out. We get a lot of objections to what we consider details, not unimportant details, but details. At the end of *Golden Spiders*, there is a scene where Archie comes down and gives Mrs. Drossos half of the fee, and there is actually dialogue between her and Archie. It's not in the book. No one said a thing so we decided to start taking more liberties because people were letting us get away with it. Sharon wrote some scenes with Lily Rowan. There were lots of reasons why we did.

What distinguishes this series from any other that has been on the air is that we use only author-written material, and we chose early on to use a repertory of actors so you'll see many of the same actors come back and play multiple roles. That's worked out for us because a lot of actors come from the be-a-ciga-rette school of acting, every thing is very dramatic. It's really hard to find actors who just have fun with the material so when we do, and we put a lot of energy into finding them, we try to do just that.

A BLACK ORCHID TOAST

by Isaac Asimov

(1ˢᵗ *published in the* Rex Stout Journal *# 7, Autumn 2001*)

It came upon December 6
In that glorious year of old
When logic, humor, and genius mix
Producing an infant of gold.
Oh, Rex is king and Stout means fat
And Nero is both of these
From Fer-de-lance to Family Affair
May his glory never decrease

[*John McAleer's Editor's Note: At the Wolfe Pack's 3rd Annual Black Orchid Banquet, I had occasion to sit next to Isaac Asimov. Isaac was familiar with the* Rex Stout Journal, *so I asked him if he would be willing to write a toast for the Journal celebrating Nero, Archie, and Rex. To my surprise he authored the toast right at the table on the back of his invitation card. Upon arriving home I placed the precious toast in a "safe" place and did not discover it until a few months ago. Henceforth, let no one question the author's love for Nero, Archie, and Rex.*]

[*Additional note by Andrew McAleer: My father would likely have discovered this Asimov toast during the spring of 2001 and then published it in the Autumn 2001 RSJ, which is the last RSJ to be published and the last one edited by him.*]

STOUT ON STOUT

from the massaranduba desk of
Andrew McAleer

Editor's Note: Archie's check-writing table was made out of massaranduba wood (a Brazilian species). Rex purchased it from Henry Ford in 1930.

ARMCHAIR mystery connoisseurs (Nerophiles in particular) may find it difficult to believe that my father, John McAleer, missed out on some great Stoutian wit in his Edgar winning biography, *Rex Stout*.

In the 1963 *Celebrity Register*, Rex Stout offers up his own stouthearted philosophy.

In the satisfactory column he reports: "I love books, food, music, sleep, people who work, heated arguments, the United States of America, and my wife and children."

In the pfui column he adds: "I dislike politicians, preachers, genteel persons, people who do not work or are on vacation, closed minds, movies, loud noises and oiliness."

Back in his office I reported the oversight to my father. He laced his fingers, leaned in his chair, and began pursing his lips.

I swiveled.

THE WOLFE PACK

IN CHOOSING selections about The Wolfe Pack for this section of *The Nero Wolfe Files,* I tried to strike a balance between necessary history and the ephemeral.

How things began was a logical choice, but the details of memorable Pack outings such as our visits to Rex Stout's home, High Meadow, struck me as chiefly significant as memories to those who attended. The annual meetings always culminate in the Black Orchid Banquet, so that has been represented both for historical reasons and in hopes of attracting new members. On the afternoon of the "BOB" there is always an excellent Assembly conducted by Ettagale Blauer in which papers on topics of Neronian/Stoutly interest are read. Quite a few of the *Gazette* articles in this collection began as Assembly presentations. Other events such as the Shad Roe dinners and Brunch Hunts (in which Pack members who wish to play are given clues and try to be the first to arrive at the restaurant), fun though they are, are not represented, though a sampling of Shad Roe limericks has been included in the Appendices.

For further information, see The Wolfe Pack website, http://nerowolfe.org

How The Wolfe Pack Began is in the Premier Issue (Winter 1979) of *The Gazette,* where it appears as *A Word from the Werowance.* Also in that issue are the menu and program of the first Black Orchid Banquet, with an accurate overview of the affair provided by Marjorie Mortensen, Jacques Barzun's greetings, and John McAleer's keynote address.

The Wolfe Pack has had two presidents — *werowances* — and they each provided autobiographical remarks, respectively, in the Fall 1987 *Gazette* (Volume V # 4) and the Summer 1988 edition (Volume VI # 3). The meaning and source of the term appears at the beginning of this piece.

The Winter 1987 *Gazette* (Volume V # 1) began with *A Word from the Werowance* that explained the origins of the Pack's Nero Award for outstanding mystery novels; it is included here with the complete list of award recipients from 1979 through 2003.

Despite my desire to eliminate ephemera, I could not leave out the American dinner which, in Ellen Krieger's words, may have been "The Ultimate Wolfe Pack Event." Her description of that memorable evening, its menu and program appear in the Summer 1987 *Gazette* (Volume V # 3), as does the text of Mr. Wolfe's remarks — the main reason I have included this piece. Anyone who read *Too Many Cooks* will remember that the Great Detective gave a speech in praise of American cuisine to a gathering of international chefs. Archie quotes only some of its highlights, but for the Pack's recreation of the dinner, Robert Goldsborough did an expanded version that, delivered by Henry Enberg, was to my mind the highlight of the evening.

There is a downside to the memory, however, something that has been called the curse of The Wolfe Pack, and the details are provided by Ettagale Blauer in *Death of a Diner,* from a Special Commemorative Edition of *The Gazette* in December 1997, which was the Pack's twentieth anniversary.

Another special issue of *The Gazette,* Fall 1998 (Volume XII # 4), was dedicated to the memory of Henry Enberg — "Wolfean, Sherlockian, and Friend." Ruth Hazen's toast lists Henry's great ongoing contributions to The Wolfe Pack; he is deeply missed.

A LETTER FROM
THE MAYOR

THE CITY OF NEW YORK

OFFICE OF THE MAYOR
NEW YORK, N.Y. 10007

September 10, 1984

To The Wolfe Pack
Post Office Box 822
Ansonia Station
New York, New York

Greetings:

As London's Baker Street is celebrated as the home of Sherlock Holmes, so is a townhouse, complete with greenhouse, on Manhattan's West 35th Street, enshrined in the hearts of devotees of the great detective, New York City's own brilliant and irascible Nero Wolfe.

As the 50th anniversary of the publication of *Fer-De-Lance*, the first of Rex Stout's 33 novels and 39 short stories to chronicle Wolfe's cases approaches, I salute the officers and members of The Wolfe Pack who, learnedly and loyally, strive to perpetuate the most highly merited fame of Wolfe and his gifted creator.

With orchids to everyone,

Sincerely,

Edward I. Koch
Mayor

HOW THE WOLFE
PACK BEGAN

by Ellen E. Krieger, Werowance

EARLY IN 1969 [I was a mere child at the time, of course], I was
one of 614 people who entered a "Mammoth New Nero Wolfe
Contest" sponsored by The Viking Press. The contest — four
very simple questions about the Wolfe books — appeared in a
New York Times Book Review ad for William S. Baring-Gould's
Nero Wolfe of West Thirty-Fifth Street. Together with 242 other
people who correctly answered the questions, I received a certificate signed by L. T. Cramer, declaring me to be a charter member
of the West 35th Street Irregulars. I hoped that this organization
would develop into something more than a publisher's ad campaign, but nothing came of it.

Four years later, in the summer of 1973, I received a letter
from John McAleer, who was then working on his biography of
Rex Stout and wished to correspond with Wolfe fans. Since my
charter membership in the West 35th Street Irregulars was all that
officially identified me as a Wolfe fan, I surmised that McAleer
had reached me through my association with this nominal organization, and I added this P.S. to my reply:

> If any of the other people you've written to express disap-
> pointment that the West 35th Street Irregulars never amounted
> to anything beyond a promotional gimmick, I'd appreciate it if
> you could send me their addresses so I can contact — oops, I
> don't believe I said that [*Wolfe strongly dislikes this usage of the*

word 'contact' — MK] — get in touch with them. Thank you.

McAleer wrote back: "I did get your address from the W. 35th Street Irregular file.

I bombed with most of them, however . . . I'll go through my files and send you the addresses of several Stout enthusiasts who'd enjoy corresponding with you. I'm thinking of suggesting a number of topics to this `Wolfe Pack' or whatever else I'll call it ('Irregulars' is too Holmesian for my tastes)."

We now had a name if not an organization, but still nothing came of it.

Of course I'm not the only person who's flirted with the idea of organizing a group like The Wolfe Pack. John McAleer mentioned a few such groups in his speech at the Black Orchid Banquet in December (1978), and I recently read a column by Bob Wiemer in *Newsday*, a Long Island newspaper, in which he mentioned having formed something called Rusterman's Regulars several years ago, although he admitted that the Regulars have yet to hold a meeting. It would be interesting to hear from other Pack members who've been involved in precursors of The Wolfe Pack.

On November 3, 1977, Carol Brener of the Murder Ink bookstore in New York held the memorable Maitre D'tective dinner to celebrate the publication of Professor McAleer's book. [*His biography of Rex Stout — MK*] A questionnaire was distributed at the dinner to ascertain the nature and extent of any interest in forming a Wolfe Pack and to solicit volunteers to plan and run the fledgling organization. A second edition of the questionnaire was sent to people who missed the dinner but had approached Carol about the Pack. Possibly because of my intense disappointment at having been unable to attend the dinner, I volunteered my services to The Wolfe Pack in just about every capacity imaginable. As a result, in May 1978, Carol turned over to me her file on the Pack, consisting of seventy completed questionnaires and some very helpful preliminary organizational work. Nine years had passed since Viking's Mammoth New Nero Wolfe Contest and the West 35th Street Irregulars, but something was to come of it at last.

On June 6, 1978, I laid in a supply of beer and invited six total strangers to my apartment to found The Wolfe Pack. It was a congenial meeting (even though no one touched the beer) as well as a productive one (possibly because no one touched the beer). At the end, the seven of us wrote checks for $10, payable to The Wolfe Pack, turned them over to our treasurer-to-be Jim DiGiovanni, and became the Pack's first official members.

In August we launched our membership drive in earnest. We sent a mailing to the seventy questionnaire respondents, all but ten of whom have since joined the Pack. A press release went out to newspapers and magazines, book trade publications, and specialty bookstores. We haven't yet equaled Viking's 614 entrants in the Mammoth New Nero Wolfe Contest (still true, alas), but considering that we're charging a membership fee and not offering prizes, I think we can be quite pleased with our current 400-plus membership.

[This number has held steady through the years, which is pretty impressive when you consider it's been quite some time since we've had a real membership drive.]

Hearing from all my fellow Wolfeans has been an enormous amount of fun for me. We don't have enough information to do a real demographic study, but even so the diversity of our membership is impressive. There are teenagers in the Pack, and there are nonagenarians (if we have any centenarians, they haven't identified themselves). The teenagers are of course now Generation Xers, and the nonagenarians . . . well, let's not go down that path. I hesitate to start listing professions because it would be hard to know where to stop: doctors, lawyers, teachers, students, businessmen, writers, caterers, artists, editors, librarians . . . you can see my problem. We have Pack members in almost every state as well as in Canada, England, and Italy. (Our geographic boundaries have expanded since then, with members in South America, Australia, and Singapore; for a while one of our members lived in Saudi Arabia.) Some are Stout collectors and scholars and some are simply casual readers. There are mystery buffs and people who read no mysteries at all except the Wolfe books; there are long-time fans and others in the enviable position of having just discovered the books, who have the pleasure of reading them for the first time.

There is even a contingent who joined the Pack because they're madly in love with Archie Goodwin — not to mention a few who confess to being madly in love with Nero Wolfe. Of course, the categories often overlap (I'm in at least two myself, but I'm not telling which).

One of the questions we discussed at that historic June 6, 1978 meeting, and one which several people have asked me since, is: What will The Wolfe Pack do? You're holding in your hands right now one of the things that the Pack will do; elsewhere in this issue you will read Marjorie Mortensen's account of another major Pack function. Beyond the *Gazette* and the annual dinner, what The Wolfe Pack will do is really up to all of us. The activities of the Pack are limited only by the imagination, enthusiasm, and energy of its members. From what I've seen of our membership, the possibilities should be almost infinite, and I'm looking forward to sharing the excitement of these possibilities with all of you.

(Of course, in 1997 [— *when the article was first written* — MK], I could list any number of regular and once-in-a-lifetime Pack events that have become part of Wolfe Pack history — the Shad Roe Dinner, the Nero Wolfe Assembly, Nero Wolfe Award, the Brunch Hunt, the Kanawha Spa dinner, the dedication of the plaque at 454 West 35th Street, the Greenbrier weekend — that the Pack has celebrated since I wrote this article. A planned trip to Montenegro was aborted when we had insufficient subscribers, but I'm confident the Pack will visit The Black Mountain one of these days.)

NOTES ON THE FIRST BLACK ORCHID BANQUET

by Marjorie Mortensen

THE WOLFE PACK held its first event, the Black Orchid Banquet: A Family Affair, on Saturday, December 2, 1978. The scene was New York's charming Gramercy Park Hotel in the heart of Nero Wolfe country. (Archie surely stops in occasionally for a drink en route to Centre Street.)

We were afraid it would be difficult to find a place to hold the dinner, but Tom O'Brien, the hotel's banquet manager, was immediately enthusiastic and kept his good humor during the six weeks of planning and through endless questions and requests. "At the head table we need one red chair and the rest yellow," he was told. "Can all the beer be in bottles? Can the bartender save the caps?" "Please explain to the waiters that someone may die."

The evening began with cocktails in the "Flamingo Room" on the second floor overlooking Gramercy Park. To stimulate curiosity and conversation, an exhibit entitled "Doors to Death" displayed clues from several Wolfe novels. They included such sinister objects as a hot water bottle, a bath brush, a golf club, a bottle of aspirin, a stained necktie, Jordan almonds, and a box of Meltettes. (No reference will be given; Plot It Yourself).

Upon arrival each Pack member received a name tag decorated with the picture of an orchid. On the tags were the flowers'

Latin names, some of which fitted the occasion perfectly. Pola Stout received *Cattleya Rex*, John McAleer was given the Black Orchid (*coelogyne pandurata*), and Jim DiGiovanni, our treasurer, had *Dendrobium Taurinum* in honor of Caesar — and that which is Caesar's. A few of the names were more personally appropriate. The profusely bearded Bill DeAndrea, for example, wore a name tag with *Paphiopedilum Hirsutissimum*.

The greatest fun of the cocktail hour was seeing all our fellow Wolfeans for the first time, like meeting a lot of new old friends. People came from New York, New Jersey, Connecticut, Pennsylvania, Delaware, Massachusetts, Michigan, Ohio and Georgia as well as from Toronto, Canada. The farthest traveler was Gladys Booth Ohlin from Texas; the most persistent was sixteen year-old Scott Scharer. On his way down from New Hampshire, Scott missed his plane connection in Boston but did not give up. He finally arrived during dinner.

A few of the 126 guests came in character. Jill Martin wore yellow pajamas, though her slender figure made an unlikely Nero Wolfe. Larry Brooks and several other men wore yellow shirts, but none stuffed pillows inside for the full effect. A number of women came dressed in clothes from the Thirties and Forties, befitting the period of many of the stories. Shirley Clark wore a specially made black orchid, while Tenby Storm and Marion Wilson appeared with bloody bullet holes neatly centered on their foreheads.

At 7:30 p.m. we trooped downstairs to the "Fritz Brenner Room" where each table was adorned with a Black Orchid set in yellow tissue in a Red Box. (After searching in vain for orchids, I made the centerpieces from black silk lilies; the man from whom I bought them turned out to be a Nero Wolfe fan and was thrilled to hear how they were to be used!) Yellow menus, topped by a black *Cattleya Rex*, listed the dishes with their relevant quotes. Each person also received two lapel buttons suitable for all occasions. "Satisfactory" was printed on one, and "Pfui" on the other.

The delicious dinner was prepared from recipes in *The Nero Wolfe Cookbook*. Chef Desi Giacaz did a fine job of interpreting quantities and flavors for a much larger group than ever dined in the old brownstone. Each dish was worthy of Wolfe's table. Guests especially enjoyed the Poached Eggs Burgundian and Fritz's Salad with Devil's Rain Dressing. And, whether it was the effect of the white wine or the general good feeling, no one questioned the blueberry-fedness of the chicken.

As the meal began, distinguished guests and officers of The Wolfe Pack read favorite selections from the books. Carol Brener set the mood with the first paragraph from the first novel, *Fer-de-Lance*. Other readers included cartoonist Gahan Wilson, declaiming the mouth-watering Kanawha Spa speech in great Wolfean form, writer Nancy Winters (Mrs. Gahan Wilson), mystery writers Chris Steinbrunner and Marvin Kaye; Eleanor Sullivan, editor of *Ellery Queen's Mystery Magazine*, and Barbara Burn, Rex Stout's last editor at Viking. (If I were Barbara, my favorite quote would be "Barbara Burn's name should be on the title page," from Rex Stout's acknowledgements in *The Nero Wolfe Cookbook*). Otto Penzler, publisher and proprietor of The Mysterious Press, read one of Wolfe's cynical comments on women, while his fiancee looked at him somewhat cynically.

While dinner progressed, the mirrored columns of the "Fritz Brenner Room" reflected heads bent in consultation over the contents of the sealed envelope found on each table. Inside each envelope was a quiz and an invitation to write a theme song for a specific book. Laughter and secretive humming sounds soon mingled with the clink of glasses and silverware. It was clear that people were getting along well and really liking each other. One table formed such instant, warm friendships that they formally requested the Miss Congeniality Award!

Whenever a song was ready, water glasses were tapped for attention and everyone at the table stood up and sang. One of the high spots was Bill DeAndrea's tenor soulfully pealing above the other voices: "Six unwed mothers at the Grantham ball . . ." These lyrics for *Champagne for One* brought down the house, but as a Casablanca devotee, I'm afraid that Dooley Wilson's version of "As Time Goes By" will never again bring tears to my eyes after such an irreverent adaptation. Loud applause also greeted a heroic response to the challenge to write a song for *Curtains for Three*. The dauntless Wolfeans at that table not only invented a verse for each story, but a wrap-up verse as well!

In the midst of these festivities a loud cry rang out. A distinguished-looking man jumped to his feet, clutching his throat. He staggered, gasped, and dropped to the floor. The woman seated next to him cried out in alarm and horrified waiters ran up. The youngest guest, fifteen-year-old Alexandra Franklin, immediately ran over and pressed his fingernail. "Dead!" she pronounced. A moment of silence — then cheers and applause, as the corpse shook with laughter. After the murder method was outlined — a poisoned pill in a pillbox full of ordinary tablets — a chorus of voices immediately called out, "Home to Roost." The marvelous "victim" and his wife were Bill and B. Jo Farley from Michigan. They had sent a delightful note with their dinner reservation and I wrote back inviting them to perform a murder with the following limitations: no real weapons, no real death, no spilling, and don't scare the waiters. I got no reply, but when the Farleys entered the "Flamingo Room" I looked warily at Bill and muttered, "Do you have anything to tell me?" His eyes lit up with an evil twinkle. "We have a few ideas to discuss," he said. Later the Farleys told me that when they received my letter, "We knew immediately that you were a nut!" Their performance during the "murder" was so convincing that it made the waiters forget all previous warnings to disregard anything. And special praise to Alexandra, who hadn't been forewarned but who immediately picked up Archie's role.

After the cherry tarts and coffee had been served, Ellen Krieger read a greeting from Jacques Barzun, who could not be present [*His statement is the next item in this book* — MK]. She then introduced John McAleer, who entertained us with a humorous and informative address. John, an integral part of the Stout and Wolfe families, is always delightful with his first-hand anecdotes of Rex Stout and his intimate knowledge of the works.

GREETINGS TO THE WOLFE PACK

by Jacques Barzun

GREETINGS TO The Wolfe Pack! Now that this group of well-tuned spirits has been formally established, it is good to recall that it has flourished implicitly for forty-four years — ever since *Fer-de-Lance* appeared in 1934. It is certainly a record for so large a society to keep its secret so well that not even its members knew it existed. But from this day forward we are out in the open, and I am confident that the household at West 35th Street welcomes us all — certified wolves, wolverines, and guests, whom we should call sheep in Wolfe's clothing.

The occasion ought perhaps to be marked by a bit of ritual. I would suggest as the formula for opening the yearly ceremonial, and also as the token of membership for newcomers, the reciting of a verse in the form of a clerihew, the form invented by another great master of crime fiction, E. C. Bentley. I therefore submit to your approval these simple, but evocative lines:

> *Rex Stout*
> *Never had the slightest doubt*
> *He could make a hero*
> *Of a man called Nero.*

— November 21, 1978

A WELCOME TO THE WOLFE PACK

by John McAleer

(Address delivered at The Black Orchid Banquet. December 2, 1978)

THIRTEEN MONTHS AGO, on November 3, 1977, at the Maitre D'tective dinner at the Lotos Club in New York, Carol Brener, sovereign mistress of Murder Ink, suggested that the time had come for Stout fans to organize The Wolfe Pack. Our presence here tonight proves once again that Victor Hugo was right when he said, "Nothing is so powerful as an idea whose time has come." So to all of those who worked so hard to bring this moment to pass, our debts are mountain high. (Which mountain? Why the Black Mountain, of course!)

Rex Stout often told me that he did not care if he himself was forgotten, so long as Wolfe and Archie were remembered. Rex was being characteristically generous. If we took him at his word and ignored him, as the Baker Street Irregulars ignore Doyle, we would not only be wanting in gratitude, but we would also be impoverishing ourselves.

As Mark Van Doren has pointed out, the identities of Rex Stout, Nero Wolfe and Archie Goodwin are inextricably intertwined. This is reason enough for my urging you tonight to give The Wolfe Pack the kind of significance Rex Stout would have wanted.

We must now ask ourselves, "Why have we come together as The Wolfe Pack?" I could say that we were in need of an elegant excuse to work our way through the recipes in *The Nero Wolfe*

Cookbook. As the plates we have emptied tonight attest, that is not in itself an unworthy goal. Yet hundreds of people who could not attend this dinner have joined The Wolfe Pack. Ellery Queen, Agatha Christie, Dorothy Sayers, John Dickson Carr and many other writers of detective fiction all have loyal bands of adherents. Hundreds, perhaps thousands, more are enrolled in courses on the detective story currently being offered at some 600 American colleges and universities. There is even a Cliffs Notes Detective in Fiction study guide for (heaven help us) students unable to follow the plots of detective stories on their own.

We must therefore pose a second question: Why do people read detective stories? Rex Stout once suggested that it is because these stories support the illusion that man is a rational animal. Somerset Maugham thought the reason was that people like well-made tales. Maugham's own fictions are well-made. Who reads them now? They are the dregs of every used-book sale. On a somewhat loftier plane, Howard Haycraft says the detective story is a phenomenon of the democratic world. It flourishes only in countries where justice is possible, in proportion to the strength of the democratic tradition and the essential decency of nations. Charles Brady thinks the detective story offers a fixed point of moral order in an increasingly relativistic universe. To W. H. Auden it is a form of Grail quest, to Charles J. Rolo, a blood-stained fairy tale which reenacts the cycle of Paradise Found, Paradise Lost, Paradise Regained.

Perhaps the best explanation is the one given by Edgar Allan Poe, progenitor of the detective story. Poe wrote that detective fiction is admired because it exercises the mind in the pursuit of its natural object, truth. Rex Stout liked that idea, which isn't surprising. Rex was fiercely dedicated to those truths mankind must live by if civilization is to survive. It was Rex who caused Nero Wolfe to say in "Door to Death:" "It would be foolhardy to assume that you would welcome a thorn for the sake of such abstractions as justice or truth, since that would make you a rarity almost unknown." Nero Wolfe is such a man, and so was Rex Stout.

No one knew this better than Mark Van Doren, Rex's closest friend for forty years. "Rex knew that the detective story must remain civilized, and the detective remain a gentleman," Prof. Van Doren once told me. "That is what the literature of detection is all about: the protection of civilization by those courageous and competent enough to save it." At one time the hard-boiled detective story, with its anti-establishment bias, threatened the dissolution of the genre. Van Doren held that Rex Stout saved the day by effecting a fusion of the best elements of the hard-boiled school with those of the classical tradition. Nicolas Freeling, creator of Inspector Van der Valk, agrees. Through Nero Wolfe, Freeling has said, Rex is a "very staunch exponent of the values traditionally upheld throughout Western civilization."

Edmund Crispin, whose death we currently mourn, has expounded on the same point. "Wolfe is prepared to do battle personally with the entire resources of the State," says Crispin. "In a world where most citizens regard such battles as lost even before begun, Wolfe is a citizen who still wins them, and would regard it as wholly contemptible to refuse their challenge, let alone delegate the fighting to some organization. Wolfe is needed by us not just for detecting, but for the fact that in testing his mettle against Authority he reminds us that we ought much more often to be testing ours."

During his lifetime Rex Stout sold one hundred million copies of his books. At his death he had fifty-seven books in print, more than any other living American writer. Rex has no narrow following. His readers range from teenagers to nonagenarians, from car hops to heads of state. Dwight Eisenhower, Anthony Eden, Giscard d'Estaing and Hubert Humphrey all have admired his work. So have numerous writers including Graham Greene, P. G. Wodehouse, Henry Miller, Mary Stewart, Robert Penn Warren and William Faulkner. Scholars, churchmen and scientists have all read Stout's books with pleasure. So, too, have artists like Marlene Dietrich, Rene Magritte, Orson Welles and John Wayne. As charter members of The Wolfe Pack we are the active nucleus of a readership entitled to expect great things of us, even as it expected great things of the man whose achievements we celebrate.

Where do we go from here? Not long ago *The New York Times* called Nero Wolfe, "purer even than Sherlock Holmes." The moment was at hand, the *Times* added, for students of the Wolfe canon to assess it in earnest — yet another idea whose time, we think, has come. To be sure, we have challenges to face. Inevitably we shall be compared to the Baker Street Irregulars. With all due respect to Holmes and Watson, whom many of us admire even as Rex himself did, I think we can do better.

Let us begin by considering three questions. What would Rex Stout frown upon? What would he tolerate? What would he warm to? From the answers I hope we may sense the direction in which we must move. To begin with: Would Rex have discouraged the formation of a Wolfe Pack? No. Rex was delighted when an active fan club sprang up in Syracuse, N.Y., even to the point of acting as godfather — though not in the Brando sense. He also authorized a gaggle of Princeton undergraduates to found a Black Orchids chapter on campus. (You see, we've been anticipated, though I doubt if they eat as well as we do.) Rex found fan mail time-consuming, but conceded — with just the right show of reluctance — that he welcomed it anyway because "self-esteem is a glutton." He couldn't bring himself to write his autobiography. "Any man who writes one thinks too damn much of himself," he said, yet he hugely enjoyed being the subject of a biography.

Rex would not want his Wolfe gang (how did Mozart get in there?) to be elitist, sexist, racist or factional by pitting itself against the Holmes Society, the Sayers Society or the Christie Caucus. Nor would he want it to be smug, pretentious, self-congratulatory, reactionary or glum. He would hate a Wolfe Pack journal that overflowed with academic jargon or preoccupied itself with nit-picking. Not for him such quibbles as why Archie doesn't use the possessive case when he says, in *Too Many Clients*: "Sometimes they heard footsteps in the hall, and they had always sounded like women."

It's likely, too, that Rex would have small patience with parody scholarship that wonders, for example, "Did Sherlock Holmes father Nero Wolfe in 1891 during an interlude of dalliance with Lizzie Borden?" "Are Tarzan and Wolfe ortho-cousins?" (Where else in America can 126 people be found in one room who all know what an ortho-cousin is?) Most emphatically, Rex would not care to see a Wolfe publication that is badly edited or hastily proofread. Probably he would enjoy one that builds the vocabularies of subscribers by introducing into each issue a few unfamiliar yet functional words. I hereby suggest "concinnity," "commorantic," and "flocculent."

Above all, Rex would sneer at attempts to continue the saga with, let us say, *Nero Wolfe Goes to Hawaii, Nero Wolfe Meets the Creature from the Black Lagoon,* or even *Son of Nero Wolfe.* "Let them roll their own," he told me when I asked him how he would look upon such ventures. Pastiches are another matter. Rex was entertained by Lawrence Meyer's *Washington Post* sequence depicting Wolfe, in the peak phase of the Watergate hearings, grilling Richard Nixon in the very office where so many other malefactors have heard their doom pronounced.

As for the things Rex would tolerate, I don't think he would object to the founding of regional chapters of The Wolfe Pack which could meet several times each year and give those who cannot attend the annual meetings a chance to swap views, information, surmises, and maybe an occasional recipe or orchid tuber. He would doubtless approve of active letter writing among members of the Rubber Band, the Buried Caesars, the Silent Speakers, so as to alert one another to opportunities to supplement their Stout collections or to allusions to the Wolfe saga found in the books of other authors, or to a mention of Wolfe, or Archie, or Rex himself, in the *New York Times* crossword puzzle.

I think he would bear with us while we celebrated Wolfe's birthday on October 18th, Archie's birthday on October 23rd, and Rex Stout's birthday on December 1st. He might even look the other way while members concocted a Nero Wolfe calendar, a Nero Wolfe Quiz Book, or issued an annual volume containing the best critical papers read at their meetings. Certainly he would find acceptable study sessions in which Wolfe fans read the great books that Wolfe admired: LaRochefoucauld, Montaigne, Erasmus, Polybius, Jane Austen, and Macaulay. Those who sought to clarify puzzling points in the stories or elaborate intriguing details, such as a rundown on Prohibition beer, might even rate a slight nod of acquiescence. And what about those who want to lobby for a Nero Wolfe TV series? Rex said that would be all right, but only after he was dead because then he wouldn't have to look at it.

We come now to the things that Rex would approve. He would want us to discuss his stories in a spirit of camaraderie. To exchange insights with gusto. To enter enthusiastically into the business of finding for one another the books we need to complete our collections, of spreading the gospel of Nero Wolfe to the enlightened — in a word, recruitment. He would relish campaigns to get libraries to stock the entire saga. A library I visited this past week listed thirty-two Wolfe books in its card catalogue. Two were on the shelves. The others, the librarian explained, had been "read to pieces." Replacement copies were not available. What does that mean for the future reputation of the stories? Rex would welcome a campaign to get Viking to bring out the complete saga in a uniform edition. After all, hasn't Dodd & Mead just issued volume 24 in its matched set of Agatha Christie? I should add that something of the kind may be forthcoming. A Penguin series which would include all the titles now published by Pyramid and Bantam, with special packages in slipcases, is currently on the drawing board.

Once the need was explained to him, I think Rex would welcome publication of a complete Stout bibliography listing all his works in all editions. At least I hope he would, since I have been asked lately to co-edit such a volume for publication a year hence. I think Rex would rejoice in stimulating discussions centered around book-length critiques of the Wolfe saga being written by Richard Reis, Guy Townsend, Colin Graham, and, yes, myself. (By the way, this coming spring, Studio Press, a subdivision of Viking, is bringing out a photographic essay on High Meadow in a book entitled, *Homes of Famous Authors*).

I think Rex would be glad to have us list the major university collections of detective fiction to ascertain the present state of their Stout holdings and learn what we can do to add to them. Having recently been appointed official archivist of the Mystery Writers of America, I am pleased that I personally will be making such inquiries. I might add that Rex was warmly gratified in 1973 when Jim Marvin, director of the public library in Topeka, Kansas (Rex's home town), announced that the new library's elegant Topeka Room would one day house the world's most complete Stout collection, a goal now well on its way to realization.

In a day when publishers claim that interest in detective fiction is waning, I am certain Rex would take satisfaction in knowing that a howling, ravenous Wolf e Pack is communicating, loud, and clear, the message that this just isn't so. One way to do this is to act on Ellen Krieger's suggestion that the Pack bestow, at its annual banquet, a meaningful Nero Wolfe Award intended to honor those bringing distinction to the genre.

Finally, whatever we are up to — reading, discussing, collecting, writing, quizzing, investigating, campaigning or even eating — Rex would want us to have fun. Enjoyment colored everything Rex did. It is most evident in the Nero Wolfe stories and from there it has spilled over into tonight's activities. Rex would say: "Whatever Goddamn thing else you do, have fun!" And that's my wish for you.

FACSIMILE OF THE MENU OF THE 1ST WOLFE PACK BANQUET

THE WOLFE PACK PRESENTS
The Black Orchid Banquet

A FAMILY AFFAIR

Saturday, December 2, 1978

The Gramercy Park Hotel

New York City

COCKTAILS IN THE FLAMINGO ROOM

DINNER IN THE FRITZ BRENNER ROOM
(at 902, 914, 918 or 924 West 35 Street)

Poached Eggs Burgundian

"There is one man who is more allergic to a woman in this house than he is and you are it . . . Don't worry, this woman is allergic to a man in her house. As for the eggs, poach them — you know, in red wine and bouillon —"

"Burgundian."

"That's it."

— *Death of a Doxy*

Onion Soup

"I had never really understood Wolfe's relapses . . . Nothing that I could say made the slightest dent on him. While it lasted he acted one of two different ways: either he went to bed and stayed there, living on bread and onion soup . . ."

— Fer-de-Lance

Chicken with Mushrooms and Tarragon

"The flavor of a four-months-old cockerel, trained to eat large quantities of blueberries from infancy, and cooked with mushrooms, tarragon and white wine . . . is not only distinctive, it is unique, and it is assuredly haute cuisine."

— Too Many Cooks

Broccoli

"A moving car is no place to give Wolfe bad news, or good news either for that matter, and there was no point in spoiling his dinner, so I waited until after we had finished with the poached and truffled broilers and broccoli . . . "

— Fourth of July Picnic

Fritz Brenner's Salad with Devil's Rain Dressing

"Sure, the pheasant was good enough for gods if there had been any around, and so was the suckling pig, and the salad, with a dressing which Fritz calls Devil's Rain . . ."

— Poison a la Carte

Cherry Tarts

"Fritz was making cherry tarts; a pan was just out of the over and I nabbed one and stuffed it in and darned near burned my tongue off."

— Fer-de-Lance

White Wine

"Wine was out because it put Americans to sleep and we wanted them wide awake. We were about ready for the usual compromise — a couple of bottles of white . . ."

— Prisoner's Base

Coffee

The upper left corner of the original menu had a sketch of an orchid, presumably black; it was named *Cattleya Rex*.

The evening's program was listed at the bottom of the menu:

A WELCOME TO WOLFE PACK MEMBERS
by Ellen Krieger

REX AS NERO: REX AS ARCHIIE
by John McAleer, Author of Rex Stout: A Biography

READINGS FROM THE WORKS BY DISTINGUISHED GUESTS

THEME SONGS   A QUIZ
SURPRISES

ELECTION OF OFFICERS

Dinner Chairman: *Marjorie Mortensen*

WHO'S WHO IN THE WOLFE PACK —

The Two Werowances

When I got back to the room, Wolfe was already behind his paper again. I felt muscle-bound and not inclined to settle down, so I said to him, "You know, Werowance, that's not a bad idea —"

A word he didn't know invariably got him. The paper went down to the level of his nose. "What the devil is that? Did you make it up?"

"I did not. I got it from a piece in the *Charleston Journal*. Werowance is a term that was used for an Indian Chief in Virginia and Maryland. I'm going to call you Werowance instead of Boss as long as we're in this part of the country . . ."

— *Too Many Cooks*

1. *An Autobiographical Sketch of Werowance Ellen Krieger*

I WAS BORN in East Orange, New Jersey, a fact I've found hard to reconcile with my longtime fantasy that I am actually the child of fabulously wealthy, aristocratic parents and was accidentally switched in the hospital with an infant of humbler stock. What I've never been able to figure out is how my fabulously wealthy, aristocratic mother happened to be giving birth in East Orange, New Jersey, at 6:40 AM on June 11, 1943.

In truth, I am proud to acknowledge my real-life biological links to the family in which I grew up, who are still among my favorite people in the world. I am the second child in a family of four daughters — two sets of girls two years apart, with a five year gap between the two sets; the sets doomed to be referred to, well into adulthood, as "the big girls" and "the little girls." We are, at least on paper, a literate family; both my parents worked in publishing, my older sister is a reference librarian, I am a children's book editor, my next younger sister edits the publications of a trade association, and my youngest sister (who does the calligraphy on the menus for many Wolfe Pack events) is an archivist.

I grew up in a variety of New York suburbs apparently chosen by my parents for their good school systems and hardy crabgrass. I was, although the term seems inappropriate for someone totally lacking athletic ability, something of a tomboy. My friends and I did play with dolls, but we didn't play mother-and-baby games; instead we directed our dolls in an assortment of adventures and melodramas of our own creation. This was, fortunately, back when dolls had flat feet, thick waists, and no boobs — before the days of Barbie and Ken. I shudder to think what sort of scenarios we would have concocted for them.

My youthful reading tastes were not terribly eclectic. I read what I had to for school, and then I read mysteries: the wholesome, respectable ones by ladies with three names — Augusta Hewell Seaman and Helen Fuller Orton — which I could find in the local library, but mostly the series, which had to be purchased with my own meager allowance or smuggled in by a friend's mother who worked in a more — or perhaps less — progressive neighboring library — Trixie Belden, the Dana Girls, and of course Nancy Drew, who was still driving her roadster in those days, and keeping Ned Nickerson at respectful distance. I remained faithful to Nancy long after I grew irritated by the contradictions in her life — she was sixteen (eighteen in some of the later books) and brilliant, but never set foot in a school, except for some art classes she took in one book — and by her unrelenting perfection. I remember one book in which the plot revolved briefly around a seeming misjudgment that Nancy made; the chapter was entitled "Nancy's 'Mistake'," with the 'mistake' in quotes to insure that the reader wouldn't for a moment believe Nancy actually capable of error.

I don't recall precisely when I graduated from juvenile to adult mysteries. I do remember being drawn to my grandfather's complete set of Philo Vance mysteries — their uniform black covers with the bright colored titles on the spines having a reassuringly familiar "series" look — but I also remember being completely bored and mystified by the odd dialect, and abandoning on the first page my attempt to read the books. The Nero Wolfe books, along with Ed McBain's 87th Precinct novels, were the first adult mysteries I remember sharing with my family. My current set of Wolfe books is a three-generation collection; some of my books are twenty-five cent and thirty-five cent paperbooks with wonderfully lurid covers, inherited from my grandfather (I have his Philo Vances now, too) and father. Nero Wolfe was definitely A Family Affair — four members of my immediate family (I, my father, and two of my sisters) were charter members of The Wolfe Pack.

Meanwhile, back in my misspent youth, I managed to tear myself away from detective fiction just enough to achieve a reasonably successful high school record and get into the college of my choice. Since my mother was a Wellesley graduate who added her encouragement to that of the Ridgewood High School guidance department, and I was a typical Eisenhower-era kid who pretty much did what I was told, that's where I ended up. I emerged, remarkably unscathed, four years later with that most useless of degrees, an AB in English Literature. I had also acquired a smattering of culture, a taste for alcohol, and a healthy vocabulary of four-letter words, all of which turned out to be considerably more useful in my chosen field of publishing.

[One of the founders of The Wolfe Pack, Ellen served as its werowance for many years before ceding the job to Jonathan Levine. Still an active voice on the steering committee, Ellen is an editor at Simon& Schuster. —MK]

II. *An Autobiographical Sketch of Jonathan Levine*

BRED (AND BUTTERED) in Peekskill, New York (about forty miles north of New York City and fifteen miles west of Lily Rowan's summer home), I grew up a fairly normal (believe it or not) child.

During my pre-teen years I switched allegiances from one corpulent detective, Freddy the Pig, to another, Mr. Wolfe. Proving that everything comes full cycle, today I am a member of Friends of Freddy, a literary society which follows the exploits of Walter R. Brooks' most famous creation.

I can recollect that my seminal experience with the exploits of Mr. Wolfe and his cohorts was an original edition of *Too Many Cooks* that I read upon the recommendation of my mother. From the first I was mesmerized by Mr. Stout's characterization and plotting and devoured all of the Nero Wolfe books that were available in the local library. I can still remember the joy of finding a new Nero Wolfe mystery being serialized in the *Saturday Evening Post*. Even as late as the 1970's I was thrilled at "discovering" *Death of a Dude*, a new Nero Wolfe mystery, at the Donnell branch of the New York City Public Library.

Not being a saver, alas, I regret that I have gone through three sets of Nero Wolfe books including the first edition *Too Many Cooks* with the recipes printed in the back. There is one set in the Williamstown, New Jersey, high school library, and most of one at the St. Lawrence University library. I gave away these books because "I have read them enough times so I won't want to read them again." (If you think that is a sad story, ask me about the co-op I didn't buy in 1974.)

Not a charter member of the Wolfe Pack, I was, however, one of the few who in 1969 received certificates of membership in the West 35th Street Irregulars. I first learned of the Wolfe Pack in 1979 while serving on jury duty with Tony Mann (now you know there is at least one person who has something good to say about our judicial system) and joined immediately. My pet Wolfean peeve is the current practice of many Pack members who refer to

Mr. Wolfe as Nero. PFUI! This privilege is reserved for a very select group of intimates and only a witling could be this presumptuous.

Along with my activities in the Wolfe Pack (I am currently treasurer [*I. E., at the time this appeared in The Gazette — MK*] and a member of the Steering Committee) I am on the Advisory Board of the International Chili Society, write a column for the Chili Society newspaper, am a contributing editor for *Friends of Wine* magazine, and am co-director of the largest wine tasting group in New York City. These diversions keep me pleasantly occupied and sated.

I have tried to combine two of my hobbies by naming my chili team "Nero Wolfe's Mysterious Manhattan Chili," and have entered cookoffs under this rubric in various states. The fact that I did not win the 1987 North Dakota State Cookoff or the 1985 Connecticut Cookoff, can only be attributed to the fact that the judges were all relatives of Lieutenant Rowcliff. I also coordinate the New York State Chili Cookoff and have judged at cookoffs from Florida to North Dakota, and from Massachusetts to California. If any member of the Wolfe Pack is interested in joining the International Chili Society, please make contact with me and I will send you the necessary information.

As anyone who's read my articles on wine in *The Gazette* (Vol. 11, No. 2, Vol. III, No. 4, and Vol. IV, No. 3) should be able to deduce that I am an active oenophile. Besides writing for *Friends of Wine* magazine, I have written for several other major wine publications on wine and/or spirits. So far I have been fortunate enough to visit vineyards and/or distilleries in Scotland, France, Spain, Portugal, California, and Brazil. I also coordinated the 1987 New York State Bloody Mary Mix-off, and have an interest in single malt scotch.

While wine, chili, and The Wolfe Pack are what keep the soul and spirits together, my job with the New York City Board of Education pays the rent. For the past eleven years I have served as the Executive Assistant to one of the thirty-two locally elected School Boards within NYC. As such, I do not work for the Superintendent of Schools, but serve as the staff person to the members of an elected board. From 1968 to 1977 (with one year off to finish a doctorate) I was a lecturer and later an assistant professor of education at Hunter College. My academic specialty was Social Foundations of Education and my research interest was in the politics of education. (I am still one of the city's leading experts on the NYC school board elections process. I was the primary author of several papers for education journals on school boards, school board elections, and the politics of education (writing about wine, chili, or Mr. Wolfe, however, is much more interesting and enjoyable).

I received my doctorate in education from the University of North Dakota in 1972. Prior to entering the doctoral program, I taught social studies at Williamstown High School in Williamstown, New Jersey. Before deciding to become legitimate, I spent a year doing sales promotional work for a Florida land company.

In a previous incarnation — before my interest in chili and wine matured — I helped write three books on movies and was a well regarded tournament bridge player.

As Archie might say, it is now time for me to get off my fundament and go back to work.

[*Happily for Jonathan, a few years ago he retired from education and now is happily able to devote himself untiringly to The Wolfe Pack, chili and wine, though perhaps not in that order* — MK]

THE NERO AWARD'S ORIGINS

by Ellen Krieger

SOMETIME in the first year of the Wolfe Pack's existence, the Steering Committee (which wasn't known as the Steering Committee in those days, having very little to steer at the time) decided that the Pack should give out an award. The enthusiasm and the professional credentials that we brought to this endeavor were somewhat reminiscent of Mickey Rooney and Judy Garland saying, "Hey kids, let's put on a show!" but we were getting bored sitting around waiting for steerable things to materialize.

We consulted with John McAleer, who volunteered to serve as Chairman of the Award Committee, and then put together an impressive panel of judges: Dan Andriacco, author of the *Cincinnati Post* "Mysteries" feature; Allen B. Crider, professor and authority on crime fiction; Margaret Farrar, for many years crossword puzzle editor of *The New York Times* and the widow of John Farrar, Rex Stout's original publisher; Robert Goldsborough, at that time editor of *The Chicago Tribune Sunday Magazine*, and Barbara Stout, librarian and Rex Stout's elder daughter.

We then sent a release to about forty publishers, requesting submissions for what we defined as an award for "the mystery novel published during the current calendar year which best typifies those standards set by Rex Stout, the creator of Nero Wolfe." We deliberately left the definition broad in order to attract a wide variety of titles, but this was a mistake. Most of the publishers that responded seemed to specialize in paperback original thrillers featuring lots of blood and/or scantily attired females on the covers. With a few adjustments and some prodding, we eventually started getting submissions worthy of an award bearing Nero Wolfe's name. At the 1979 Black Orchid Banquet, John McAleer presented the first Nero Wolfe Award to Lawrence Block, for *The Burglar Who Liked To Quote Kipling*.

Presentation of the Nero Wolfe Award soon became one of the most popular items on the Black Orchid Banquet program. Who can forget Martha Grimes' acceptance speech for *The Anodyne Necklace* in 1983? Her publisher had warned us that she was shy and would grace us with no more than a murmured "thank you;" instead we were treated to a charming and witty childhood reminiscence about stealing her brother's jelly beans.

The original award was patterned after Nero Wolfe's famous gold bookmark. Gold, of course, was well out of our budget (hell, even the Oscar isn't real gold). Ours was what is typically called in jewelry ads "goldtone metal." It was engraved with the Wolfe Pack logo, and the words "THE NERO WOLFE AWARD, Presented by The Wolfe Pack/To." The plaque was 9" by 2", fairly hefty, and far more attractive than useful.

After the supply of these awards ran out, Jamie O'Boyle had the idea of holding a competition for a new award design at the Moore College of Art in Philadelphia (fitting for him, since he is convinced that Mr. Wolfe moved to the City of Brotherly Love upon retiring — see *The Gazette*, Volume 1, Number 2). Whether or not Mr. Wolfe has forsaken The Big Apple for the City of Brotherly Love, it is unlikely that he would choose Moore College for such a competition, since it is an all-female institution. Nevertheless, Betsy Hatcher, a Moore student, captured Mr. Wolfe perfectly in the bust she designed.

Jane Langton, who won the 1984 award for *Emily Dickinson Is Dead*, received the first Nero Wolfe bust, which she described in her thank you note as "strong, powerful, and monumental, a slightly sinister portrait of a big man with a big mind." On the assumption that Martha Grimes (see *The Gazette*, Vol. III, No. 2, p. 6) is not the only early winner who feels cheated out of this work of art, the Pack has plans to award busts retroactively to the first four winners, possibly in 1988, which will mark the tenth anniversary of the award.

Through the years the Wolfe Pack has awarded the Nero to established masters like Helen McCloy, Hugh Pentecost, and Amanda Cross, as well as to talented newcomers like Dick Lochte and Bob Goldsborough. Except for the inevitable change in the panel of judges, few changes have been made in the way the award decision is made. For some time, however, the Steering Committee has wanted to involve the Pack membership directly in this process. With this goal in mind, we are instituting some changes for the 1987 award.

First, the criteria are clarified. The 1987 Nero will be given to the best detective fiction novel first published in the United States between September 1, 1986 and September 1, 1987. Also Wolfe Pack members are invited to submit nominations throughout the year. An entry form is included at the end of this article (a facsimile, or several, may be used). Nominations may be made until September 15, 1987. After all nominations are received, the Steering Committee will tabulate the entries and identify the top five titles for the judges panel. The panel will be identified in a future issue of *The Gazette*.

We're tremendously excited about this change in the process of selecting the Nero Wolfe Award. We've always felt that an award for a fine piece of detective fiction writing is an ideal way to honor the memory of Rex Stout, and under this new system all of us can participate in this honor.

[LATER HISTORY — I have omitted the entry form that followed Ellen's article because the character of the award changed since then, although nominations from Wolfe Pack members have always been solicited and honored. For several years I headed the Award Committee, working with such distinguished judges as Professor McAleer, Barbara Stout, Robert Goldsborough, who, delightfully, always seemed to share my opinion of the best submitted mysteries, Robin Winks, and often the winner for the preceding year. Eventually, I stepped down from the

assignment, and Stephannie Russo became chairperson of the Nero Award Committee, which function she still fulfills ably. Below is the complete list of Nero Award winners to date. —MK]

2004 — *Fear Itself* byWalter Mosley

2003 — *Winter and Night* by S. J. Rozan

2002 — *The Deadhouse* by Linda Fairstein

2001 — *Sugar House* by Laura Lippman

2000 — *Coyote Revenge* by Fred Harris

1999 — *The Bone Collector* by Jeffery Deaver

1998 — *Sacred* by Dennis Lehane

1997 — *The Poet* by Michael Connelly

1996 — *A Monstrous Regiment of Women* by Laurie B. King

1995 — *She Walks These Hills* by Sharyn McCrumb

1994 — *Old Scores* by Aaron Elkins

1993 — *Booked to Die* by John Dunning

1992 — *A Scandal in Belgravia* by Robert Barnard

1991 — *Coyote Waits* by Tony Hillerman

1990 — No award

1989 — No award

1988 — No award

1987 — *The Corpse in Oozak's Pond* by Charlotte MacLeod

1986 — *Murder in E Minor* by Robert Goldsborough

1985 — *Sleeping Dog* by Dick Lochte

1984 — *Emily Dickinson is Dead* by Jane Langton

1983 — *The Anodyne Necklace* by Martha Grimes

1982 — *Past, Present & Murder* by Hugh Pentecost

1981 — *Death in a Tenured Position* by Amanda Cross

1980 — *Burn This* by Helen McCloy

1979 — *The Burglar Who Liked to Quote Kipling* by Lawrence Block

THE AMERICAN DINNER

by Ellen Krieger

IF ONE were to conduct a survey of Wolfe Pack members, asking them to describe The Ultimate Wolfe Pack Event, I suspect that a majority of them would respond with, "recreating the Kanawha Spa dinner." In truth, Mr. Wolfe spent several days at the Kanawha Spa in 1937 (from Monday, April 5th until Friday, April 9th), and consumed a number of memorable meals in that time [*In Too Many Cooks* — MK]. But it was the American Dinner, which took place on Thursday, April 8th, that was the culmination of Mr. Wolfe's visit to West Virginia. It was here that he delivered his speech, "Contributions Americaines a la Haute Cuisine," and of course here that he delivered the murderer of Phillip Laszio to the authorities.

The Steering Committee had long flirted with the idea of recreating the American Dinner for the Pack membership. The lure of this meal is so strong that several years ago a few Wolfeans, having heard that the Culinary Institute of America (CIA) was reproducing the American Dinner, rented a car and ventured out into deepest Westchester, as alien a turf to them as to Mr. Wolfe, in pursuit of this gastronomic experience. Unfortunately, it turned out that our information had been a bit fuzzy, and the dinner was a private affair being hosted by a Sherlockian who apparently shared neither Baring-Gould's theory of Wolfe's parentage [ED. — which he copied from Dr. John C. Clark] nor Mr. Wolfe's reverence for guests (at least uninvited ones). We were turned away at the door, our attempt to savor Avocado Todhunter *et al.* thwarted.

With that disappointment still bitter on our tongues several years later, we decided that the perfect time for The Wolfe Pack to hold its own American Dinner would be the Spring of 1987, to commemorate the fiftieth anniversary of the actual dinner in West Virginia. Our efforts to persuade the CIA to try its hand at the menu again were unsuccessful — our many letters went unanswered — but we were fortunate to find a restaurant closer at hand that was more amenable. Club 1407, in a convenient Manhattan location, was intrigued but not intimidated by the idea and, equally important, was able to bring in the meal at a reasonable price, considering the exotic nature of some of the courses (when was the last time you tried to buy terrapin?) and the sheer volume of food. The restaurant even had a private room to turn over to us for the evening.

And so it came to pass that on Friday, April 24th, a chilly and rainy night, the sort that makes New York taxicabs vanish, forty-two Wolfe Pack members assembled at Club 1407 to enjoy the most famous meal in all detective fiction. The smart ones wore loose-fitting clothes and had gone into rigorous training for the event — either fasting for several days to build up their appetites, or gorging to stretch their stomachs (I found the latter course more compatible to my lifestyle).

Gilt letters were strung across the entrance to the room assigned to us, identifying the location of the Kanawha Spa. Over the bar, another string of gilt letters proclaimed "Les Quinze Maitres." The tables, set with crisp linen, sparkling crystal, and shining silver, looked elegant, although some might hesitate to use the word "elegant" to describe centerpieces consisting of bloodstained toques blanches pierced with knifes. The center-pieces had been the subject of great debate among members of the Steering Committee; "toque stabbing" was even on the written agenda for one of the committee meetings, although the stabbing was less of a problem than creating realistic bloodstains. Every red substance in my home that ran, imprinted, stained, or otherwise transferred color was tested (short of real blood; we drew the line there), but nothing produced results that met our demanding standards.

But I digress. Back at the dinner, once the forty-two attendees had arrived, picked up their sherry, and admired the blood-stained centerpieces, we lined up for the first event of the evening — a reenactment of the Sauce Printemps tasting that proved to be Phillip Laszio's final culinary achievement. We took a few liberties with the test: in the interest of economy (and the sensibilities of New Yorkers who pale at the idea of consuming pigeon) we used bread, not squab, for the tasting; we eliminated squab blood from the recipe; and we didn't murder anyone during the contest. Everyone was pleasantly surprised at how tasty Sauce Printemps was, in all its nine incarnations, which tasted pretty much the same to me. The best score was six out of nine, which I refuse to believe was anything other than pure luck.

The smidgen of Sauce Printemps merely whetted our appetites for the meal to follow. And what a meal it was! The chef at Club 1407 (a woman, which would not have pleased Mr. Wolfe) had diplomatically pointed out that the menu itself was somewhat uninteresting, but in her capable hands it was anything but. From the oysters baked in the shell through the pineapple sherbet, sponge cake, and cheese, each course was a delight. Of course, by the time we got to the Sally Lunn, even my well-conditioned stomach was protesting the quantities of food I was sending its way, and my palate may have been a tad numbed by the marvelous selection of wines that Jonathan Levine had chosen to accompany the meal. But there was no question that the American Dinner more than justified Mr. Wolfe's high praise for American cuisine.

We were also fortunate to be able to share Mr. Wolfe's thoughts on this subject. Of course, there is no extant copy of the full text of Mr. Wolfe's remarks from that evening, but substantial portions are reproduced in *Too Many Cooks*, and with the help of Robert Goldsborough, Archie's current literary agent, we were able to put together a reasonable version of the speech. Read by The Wolfe Pack's favorite Wolfe impersonator, Henry Enberg, the speech was a fitting conclusion to a spectacular evening. Of course the usual Wolfe Pack rituals were observed. Henry Enberg provided a maddening quiz, replete with anagrams, terrible puns, and Wolfean esoteria. Attendees provided splendid toasts to Mr. Wolfe, Archie, Fritz Brenner, and Rex Stout and, with characteristic Wolfe Pack modesty, neglected to acknowledge authorship of the texts they submitted.

There is no question that the dinner earned a resounding "Satisfactory" from all present. The job that Club 1407 did with the food so impressed the Steering Committee that we signed up the restaurant for this year's Black Orchid Banquet. [*But see Ettagale Blauer's ensuing article, "Death of a Diner"* — *MK*] And we're already thinking about other memorable meals from the Corpus we could recreate as extra special Pack events. Shad Roe Mousse Pocahontas . . . Duck Mondor . . . a Real Nero Wolfe Trout Deal . . . With a little effort, we could all achieve Wolfean girth in no time.

[Below are the program and menu of the 1987 American Dinner]

AMERICAN DINNER
Friday, April 24,1987

Club 1407 New York City

Sauce Printemps tasting

Toasts

Quiz

Reading of Mr. Wolfe's speech:
"Contributions Americaines a la Haute Cuisine"

===================================

LES QUINZE MAITRES
Kanawha Spa, West Virginia

Thursday, April 8,1937

AMERICAN DINNER

Oysters Baked in the Shell

Terrapin Maryland

Beaten Biscuits

Pan Broiled Young Turkey

Rice Croquettes with Quince Jelly

Lima Beans in Cream

Sally Lunn

Avocado Todhunter

Pineapple Sherbet

Sponge Cake

Wisconsin Dairy Cheese

Black Coffee

NV Sebastiani Brut (Oysters)

1985 Glen Ellen Chardonnay (Terrapin)

1982 Hawk Crest Cabernet (Turkey)

1986 Gan Eden Naturally Sweet Gewurztraminer (Dessert)

CONTRIBUTIONS AMERICAINES A LA HAUTE CUISINE

a recreation by Robert Goldsborough of
Nero Wolfe's speech to Les Quinze Maitres
delivered at Club 1407 by Henry Enberg

Mr. Servan, Ladies, Masters, Fellow Guests. I feel a little silly. Under different circumstances it might be both instructive and amusing for you, at least some of you, to listen to a discussion of American contributions to *la haute cuisine*, and it might be desirable to use what persuasiveness I can command to convince you that those contributions are neither negligible nor meager. But when I accepted an invitation to offer you such a discussion, which greatly pleased and flattered me, I didn't realize how unnecessary it would be at the moment scheduled for its delivery. It is delightful to talk about food, but infinitely more delightful to eat it; and we have eaten. A man once declared to me that one of the keenest pleasures in life was to close the eyes and dream of beautiful women, and when I suggested that it would be still more agreeable to open his eyes and look at them, he said not at all, for the ones he dreamed about were *all* beautiful, far more beautiful than any his eyes ever encountered. Similarly it might be argued that if I am eloquent the food I talk to you about may be better than the food you have eaten; but even that specious excuse is denied me. I can describe, and pay tribute to, some superlative American dishes, but I can't surpass the oysters and terrapin which were so recently there (Wolfe points to the table) and are now here (he rubs his stomach with a palm).

It is said that the gastronome's heaven is France, and I grant that. But the gastronome, on his way there, would do well to make a detour hereabouts. I have, for instance, eaten *Tripe a la mode Caen* at Pharamond's in Paris. It is superb, but no more so than Creole Tripe, which is less apt to stop the gullet without an excess of wine. I have eaten bouillabaisse at Marseilles, its cradle and its temple, in my youth, when I was easier to move, and it is mere belly fodder, ballast for a stevedore, compared to its namesake in New Orleans!

American cuisine owes much to the nation's heterogeneity and its regionalism. Consider for a moment the vast and splendid culinary diversity of the United States, including its three most important centers for fine cooking — New England, South Carolina, and Louisiana — the last named of which had as one of its great moments the introduction of filé powder to the New Orleans market by the Choctaw Indians of Bayou Lacombe. But that's a speech in itself. Even beyond these great areas, the land has a truly blessed gastronomic heritage. I would ask all of you this:

Have you eaten a planked porterhouse steak, two inches thick, surrendering hot red juice under the knife, garnished with American parsley and slices of fresh limes, encompassed with mashed potatoes which melt on the tongue, and escorted by thick slices of fresh mushrooms faintly underdone?

Have you sampled Missouri Boone County ham, baked with vinegar, molasses, Worcestershire, sweet cider, and herbs? On the subject of ham, which I consider to be one of the great American dishes, I should like to shift to the indescribable flavor of the finest of Georgia hams, the quality of which places them, in my opinion, definitely above the best to be found in Europe. This is not due to post mortem treatment of the flesh at all. Expert knowledge and tender care in the curing are essential, but they are to be found in Czestochowa and Westphalia even more frequently than in Georgia. Poles and Westphalians have the pigs, the scholarship, and the skill; what they do not have is peanuts.

A pig whose diet is fifty to seventy percent peanuts grows a ham of incredibly sweet and delicate succulence which, well cured, well kept, and well cooked, will take precedence over any other ham the world affords. I offer this as an illustration of one of the sources of American contributions that I am discussing, and as another proof that American offerings to the roll of honor of fine food are by no means confined to those items which were found here already ripe on the tree, with nothing required but the plucking. Red Indians were eating turkeys and potatoes before white men came, but they were not eating peanut-fed pigs. Those unforgettable hams are not gifts of nature: they are the product of the inventor's enterprise, the experimenter's persistence, and connoisseur's discrimination.

Similar results have been achieved by the feeding of blueberries to young chickens, beginning usually at the age of one week. The flavor of a four-months-old cockerel, trained to eat large quantities of blueberries from infancy, and cooked with mushrooms, tarragon, and white wine — or if you would add another American touch, made into a chicken and corn pudding, with onion, parsley, and eggs — is not only distinctive, it is unique; and is assuredly *haute cuisine*. This is even a better illustration of my thesis than the ham, for Europeans could not have fed peanuts to pigs, since they had no peanuts. But they did have chickens and blueberries, and for centuries no one thought of having one assimilate the other and bless us with the result.

But to go on, have you ever tasted Chicken Marengo? Or chicken in curdled egg sauce, with raisins, onions, almonds, sherry, and Mexican sausage? Or Tennessee Opossum? Or Lobster Newburgh? Or Philadelphia Snapper Soup? Or Cape Cod clam cakes? Or braised wild turkey with celery sauce and corn fritters? If not, these are but a few of the delights that await you here.

My own chef, Mr. Fritz Brenner, is Swiss by birth, by heritage, and by temperament. Yet Mr. Brenner, who has traveled the world, has sampled its food, and has met and talked to great chefs from more than a dozen countries, remains convinced that the haute cuisine of America is more interesting and more diverse than that of any other country on the planet. In this as in so many matters relating to fine foods, I find myself in total agreement with Mr. Brenner. Thank you.

DEATH OF A DINER

by Ettagale Blauer

WHETHER IT is a dark and stormy night or a pleasant Fall afternoon, the Wolfe Pack seems to be the kiss of death when it comes to restaurants in New York. Cafés, upscale restaurants, hotel restaurants, even Chinese restaurants get fatal cases of food poisoning after a visit from the Pack. Even in a city known to be hard on restaurants, our effect on dining places is clearly fatal. The list of restaurants that closed their doors after we were there seems unnaturally long. The following list is probably not complete, and it needs yearly updating as we continue to cut our deadly path across New York's culinary landscape.

Perhaps the closest call we have ever had was in October 1993 when we were scheduled to hold the assembly and the Black Orchid dinner at Hart's on 27th Street. It was in fact our second such event there because the food was so good. When we arrived for the assembly, the gates were locked; it seemed a bad sign. Shortly after two o'clock, some staff arrived and opened up and the program went on. But there seemed to be something not quite right. That night we enjoyed an excellent meal. As we were on our way home, Hart's closed its doors that night, never to open them again. In hindsight, it is amazing that they had enough money to buy the food for our event.

But if we were the last people to eat at Hart's, we may have been the only people to eat at the Hermitage on West 72nd Street. This unfortunate establishment was to hold a shad roe dinner for the Pack; they neglected to buy the shad roe. The dinner was held before the restaurant officially opened. Officially or otherwise, it never did open. And another one bites the dust.

Club 1407, in the heart of the fashion district, was the site of two wonderful meals, including the tasting of Sauce Printemps. The chef, a slender woman, was roundly applauded for her efforts. And then Club 1407 closed its doors and the chef moved to Washington D.C.

Shad roe dinners seem to be particularly deadly for restaurants. The list of those that succumbed to the deadly Wolfe Pack curse include Bogie's and Patzo's. Captain Nemo's not only went under after our shad roe event, it turned into a Petland Discount store, a particularly nasty turn of events. The Century Café on Times Square is remembered for being the first time we offered the `Archie' to those who don't care for shad roe. From the dryness of the bread, it seemed clear that the café made the sandwiches when the reservation was made. That did not explain, however, why the bread was dry on one side only.

Even crossing the river to Brooklyn didn't end the Wolfe Pack curse; we did in Foffe's, the site of another shad roe dinner. And the Boulevard, the site of a successful brunch hunt, closed a week before a shad roe dinner, leaving the Pack to find another home in a hurry.

Almost any Wolfe Pack event can be deadly for a restaurant. When the Pack went in search of Rusterman's, it did in Julia's Garden and the Grove Street Café. The latter reincarnated itself under new management but the deed was done.

Montenegrin dinners proved indigestible for both Dubrovnik and Portoroz. Dubrovnik was not entirely our fault, however, since it had a Dalmatian [*One of the steering committee did a cartoon of a spotted dog wearing a chef's hat — MK*] for a chef. That did seem to be asking for trouble and trouble was what they got.

Brunch hunts did in the Exterminator Chile Café and the Zip City Brewery. The sinister nature of the Pack became clear when we closed down the Sea Palace, a Chinatown landmark. It is truly unheard of for a Chinese restaurant to close — until the Wolfe Pack makes a reservation.

The die was cast right from the beginning, although that became clear only in hindsight. We did in an entire hotel, the venerable Biltmore. The Biltmore was home to several Black Orchid banquets including the near-apocryphal `Chicken Alcoa' dinner. [*It was supposed to be Chicken 'en papilotte'* — MK] And though not in the dining category, it is worth noting that the Ansonia Post Office, which houses the Wolfe Pack's post box, has moved twice in an effort to elude the deadly curse.

As we celebrate our 20th Annual Banquet, it is worth noting with awe that the Gramercy Park Hotel appears impervious to the Pack. Were it not for the Gramercy Park, we might well be dining in Central Park.

[*Ettagale later updated this all-too-true article with many more restaurant casualties* — and *the Gramercy Park Hotel itself, which did its best to fight the curse, but unfortunately at last succumbed.* — MK]

A MEMORIAL SONG PARODY

by Marvin Kaye

(Sung to the tune of *Aura Lee aka Love Me Tender*)

Let's remember Henry E.
With a lot of love.
Where's he gone? No mystery —
He's quizzing them above.
Everything re Wolfe and Holmes,
Be sure he asks about.
And I'll bet he's stumping
Dr. Doyle and Mr. Stout.

HENRY'S SONG TO MR. WOLFE

by Henry Enberg

(Sung to the tune of *The Marine Hymn*)

From the steps of 35th Street
To the sere Montana hills,
He'll detect the nation's cri-i-imes
And send megasuric bills.

After pushing in and out his lips
And consuming half a sheep
Wolfe will solve conundrums desperate
Though criminous, vile and deep.

So if Cramer and the FBI
Into saints by God are made
They will have to sit forever
At a Nero Wolfe charade

BLACK ORCHID SONG PARODIES, SHAD ROE LIMERICKS & OTHER LAMPOONS

AT EVERY major Wolfe Pack event, musical parodies are a high-light — or low point; how one views it, I suspect, depends on one's degree of sobriety. When a tableful of diners have prepared their ditty, one of them chimes a utensil against a water glass, they all rise and without benefit of pitch pipe indulge in an *a cappella* moment of fame. Prizes are not awarded; it's all done for the laughter, the groans and publication in *The Gazette*. Here's a baker's dozen of Black Orchid songs. Where possible, authors are credited, but sometimes the lyrics were printed without attribution.

1. *Holiday Song Parodies*

Sung to the tune of "O Little Town of Bethlehem"
[Book: *In the Best Families*]

O brownstone house on 35th
Your door was open wide —
O where O where is Nero Wolfe?
We never thought you'd hide.

When Pete fell into Lily's arms,
Archie was sure surprised …
It was just a Wolfe charade
That led to Zeck's demise.

> — Bob & Margaret Hughes, William, Mary Agnes & Joanne DeAndrea, Rick Myers, Chris Steinbrunner, Joyce Shiarella, Todd Holland, Tenby Storm, Margaret Herrick

Sung to the tune of "Let it Snow"

Oh, the weather outside is frightful,
But Wolfe is still insightful.
Archie has ants in his pants —
Let him dance, let him dance, let him dance.

> — Elizabeth Levy

Sung to the tune of "Adeste Fideles"

The scribe of the Corpus
Truly is a stylist.
His words capture vilest
Villains memorably.

He writes well of murder,
Orchids, beer, and women,
But here's a thing I wonder
(I hope it's not a blunder) —
Would Nero Wolfe put Archie's books
In his library?

     — Marvin Kaye

The Twelve Days of Nero

Twelve beers a-brewing
Eleven dishes simmering
Ten cops a-calling
Nine orchids blooming
Eight spices missing
Seven steps a-stooping
Six chairs of yellow
Five yellow robes
Four hours in plant room
Three call him Nero
Two ringing phones
And Fritz cooking in the pantry!

     — Authorship unrecorded

2. Songs about Specific Books

Sung to the tune of "Baby Face"
[Book: *The 2nd Confession, In the Best Families*]

Arnold Zeck! He's Wolfe's most fearsome foe ...
He's Arnold Zeck,
And he can make you such a nervous wreck,
Arnold Zeck!
He shot up Wolfe's greenhouse,
He really is a mean louse!
Arnold Zeck ... He never realized that Wolfe had stacked the
deck.

Wolfe came back to town,
Had Rackham gun him down ...
It was the end of Arnold Zeck!

— Bill DeAndrea

Sung to the tune of "Winter Wonderland"
[Book: *The Doorbell Rang*]

Doorbells ring, are you listening?
In the street, Hoover's bristling.
Wolfe is inside with Archie at his side —
Together they will foil the FBI!

Doorbells ring, are you listening?
In the street, Hoover's bristling.
J. Edgar's at the door. His finger's getting sore —
Rachel Bruner couldn't ask for anything more!

— Authorship unrecorded

Sung to the tune of "Strangers in the Night"
[Story: *"Poison a la Carte"*]

Poison a la carte — that's what she served him.
Poison a la carte — how it unnerved him.
Wolfe knew he'd be dead before the meal was through.
Arsenic it would seem the actress brought him
Caviar and cream; she really taught him
That seducing girls is not the thing to do!

Archie couldn't tell which of the beauties
Could have planned the crime so well.
But Wolfe bugged Rusterman's and
Staged a great charade
And when the tape was played
The Ten for Aristology
Learned Wolfe-ish criminology.

So when your dress is Greek and you plan murder
Revenge is what you seek — you'll get much further
If you stab him through the heart — spurn poison a la carte!

— Mary Burns, Bill DeAndrea, Jim DiGiovanni, Alex Franklin, Mary Ruth Fletcher, Andrew Hughes, Larry Jones, Bill & Marion Kulik, Elizabeth Marinelli

Sung to the tune of "Comedy Tonight"
[Book: *Too Many Cooks*]

Something for Nero
Something for Archie
Something for Kanawha Spa
A murder tonight.

Something distasteful
Something disgraceful
Something despicable
A stabbing tonight.

Something for cooks
Nothing for crooks
Bring on Saul Panzer
To hell with his looks.

What is the motive?
Must be a motive
Here is the motive wrong or right —
Motives tomorrow
Murder tonight
One ... two ... pfui!

> — Frances, James, Larry & Marsha Brooks, Henry &
> Kenneth DeKoven, Henry Hasenberg, Christopher &
> Kathleen Pardo

3. General Neronian Themes

Sung to the tune of "She'll Be Comin' Round the Mountain")

He'll be comin' round High Meadow when he comes
He'll be talkin' about his orchids, not his 'mums,
He'll be comin' round High Meadow
Not to Wolfe Pack meals, instead-o,
Where he would not be caught dead-o, when he comes.

> — Marvin & Saralee Kaye, Ellen Krieger, Sue Oehlman, others

Sung to the tune of "Side by Side"

"Oh, we don't have a barrel of money,
IRS doesn't think it's too funny
Yet you sit on your tail
Drinking your ale
Getting wide.

"Through all kinds of headaches,
What if the roof caves in?
As long as you've got corncakes,
You're in heaven again.

"When you've filled up with dumplings and marrow
You couldn't care less you're not narrow.
And you'll have to eat crow
When the feds take your dough —
And your pride."

> — Saralee Kaye

Sung to the tune of "You're Not Sick, You're Just In Love")

I buy cigars that I never smoke.
Goodwin treats me like I'm just a joke,
Then I get so mad that I start to choke,
And Wolfe is why. And Wolfe is why.
Wolfe just watches while we chase our tails,
And makes us feel that we are slow as snails,
Then he'll tell us what the case entails,
My god, it never fails, and Wolfe is why.

Oh, come on, cheer up, Cramer,
Let me file this disclaimer.
You know that Wolfe's really not that cruel.
When he starts cogitatin'
He don't care who is waitin'
Even I've wound up like a fool.
Never mind his bad manners,
When he drives you bananas,
His assists sent you to the top.
You'll just have to face the fact.
Genius is all you lack,
You're not Wolfe, you're just a cop.

> — JoannDeAndrea, Mary Agnes DeAndrea, William L. & William N. DeAndrea; Margaret Herrick, Todd Holland, Rick Meyers, Chris Steinbrunner, Joyce Shiarella, Tenby Storm

Sung to the tune of "America the Beautiful"

O Nero Wolfe, our favorite sleuth,
Please tell us true today —
Is Mister Holmes your Dad, in truth?
Did he Iren-ee lay?

O please reveal your history —
The Stout clan won't say "Boo!"
But if you'll solve this mystery,
We'll dub thee Sherlock Two!

> — Marvin Kaye

Sung to the tune of "I've Been Working on the Railroad"

I've been working on a new case
All the livelong day
Now he's ready for a relapse
Just to pass the time away,

He'll be working with his orchids
Or cooking in the kitchen with Fritz
If Archie only would stop bugging him
He'd stop having fits.

Archie, won't you go?
Archie, won't you go?
So he can get back to his chair?

Someone's in the office with Archie
Someone's in the kitchen with Fritz
Nero's on the roof with Theodore
Trying not to lose his wits . . .
And singing, "Pfui!"

> — Mary Glascock, Tony Iacco, Beth & David Levine,
> Jan & Steve Schwartz, Ann Zawistowski

Sung to the tune of "Tit-Willow"

In a brownstone on West 35th Street there dwelled
Stout fellow, Stout fellow, Stout fellow.
Each morning would find him supine in his bed
In yellow, in yellow, in yellow.
"Is it weakness of intellect, Archie?" he cried,
"Or a corned beef and rye in your little inside?
What makes you this morning confoundedly snide?"
He bellowed, he bellowed, he bellowed.
I slapped at my desk, and looked way down my nose,
Not mellow, not mellow, not mellow.
"A Genius may sit on his duff, I suppose,
His orchids, his orchids, to smell, oh.
But if you don't get busy and take on a case,
Our tax bills will break us and you'll feed your face
With french fries and burgers and beer that is base …
And Jell-O, and Jell-O, and Jell-O."

> — Barbara Burn, Marvin & Saralee Kaye, Jan & Steve Schwartz, others

IN THE SPRING when shad roe is available, The Wolfe Pack sometimes holds a shad roe dinner, despite the fact that most members opt for the alternative menu offerings. It is traditional to write and read limericks on this occasion. Here are some of the most memorable examples:

After dining one evening on shad roe
A villain dashed off on a mad row
Across the wide lake
While trying to shake
His girl friend. Gad, look at that cad row!

— Isaac Asimov

While Nero was playing with flowers
Archie would while away hours.
Orchids are silly
It's more fun with Lily
Out testing carnality's bowers.

— "Table by the Door"

The portion of roe was not meager,
Although for some more I'm not eager.
We now all are vested
With Wolfe's dish, digested.
For this we must thank Ellen Krieger.

— Phillip Paley

Shad roe is a very strange treat
It's odd in the mouth when you eat
It's little weird eggs
Without feet or legs
And it looks more like liver than meat.

— Marjorie Mortensen

I am Goodwin and I love shad roe
More than Panzer, or Cramer (my foe)
More than Nero or Fritz,
I love it to bits,
But more than L. Rowan? No, no!

— Isaac Asimov

Said Archie, "I'm so sick of shad.
In this house it's no passing fad!"
With chervil, sauté
Shallot, parsley and bay
But onion? (Wolfe called Fritz a cad!)

— Jeanne Thelwell

Said Archie to Wolfe one spring day,
"Let's take in a ball game at Shea.
You can munch on a treat —
Perhaps saucisse minuit.
We'll call it replacement gourmet."

— Saralee Kaye

Shad roe is a very odd dish:
Not poultry, not meat, scarcely fish.
The taste is quite bland,
The texture's like sand
But pressed on the tongue, it goes squish.

— Pat Dreyfus

There was a young woman from Chad
Who devoured (exclusively) shad
Her name's Madame Bovary
And it went to her ovary
And made her both fertile and bad.

— Isaac Asimov

We all miss Isaac the A
At limericks he was more than OK
Dirty or clean,
G-rated or obscene
And now they all sell on E-Bay.

> — Jonathan Levine's tribute to Isaac Asimov

AFTER ISAAC ASIMOV died, The Wolfe Pack began an annual Isaac Asimov Limerick Contest. Here are the winners from the "Montana Trout Dinner" held April 7th, 2003.

Honorable Mention — Jan and Steve Schwartz

Said Archie to Wolfe, "She's seditious.
Her behaviour is quite surreptitious.
I saw her go out
To deal with some trout
With a group that looked mighty suspicious."

Honorable Mention — Saralee Kaye

I promised I would not use "Stout"
To rhyme with the fish we call trout
So sue me — I lied.
Believe me, I tried,
But Rex I can not do without.

Third Place — Maggie Goodman

For years I've been waiting to savor
The Montana Trout Deal's "real" flavor
Brown sugar sounds weird
Not at all like James Beard
Which just proves that The Wolfe Pack is braver.

Second Place — Marvin Kaye

Concerning Montana I'm mute.
No pun comes to mind, bad or cute.
But Wolfe, to be witty,
Said, "One major city,
From all that I've heard, is a Butte."

First Place — Tenby Storm

Mr. Brenner can sometimes seem strange
When he won't let his recipes change
But we all must admit
That his meals are a hit.
That's because he's at home on the range.

And here is one final appropriate Wolfe Pack limerick —

If you want me to tell you the truth
I feel I've recaptured my youth
As we all come and meet
To drink and to eat
To honor our favorite sleuth.

— Leon Benedict (inspired by Marianne B.)

NERO WOLFE QUIZZES

(Answers are at the end of the section.)

THOUGH OTHER Wolfe Pack members contributed quizzes and puzzles to *The Gazette*, Henry Enberg was the presiding genius of Neronian brain teasers till his death in 1998, after which Tenby Storm assumed his duties. Each year they prepare quizzes of impressive difficulty for the December feast. Each table tries to solve it collectively.

The Fall 1998 *Gazette* included this quiz, compiled from "some of Henry's diabolical attempts. We offer them with no apologies."

BLACK ORCHID BANQUET QUIZ
— December 5, 1998
Dedicated to the memory of Henry Enberg

1. The murder was diabolical, but the title was polite. Name the novella.

2. Anyone who can draft a tort can solve the first part of this one, so you should also name the story that brings to mind Old Faithful.

3. The convict is vulgar; he wants you to name this novel.

4. What diamond did Pierre Mondor covet?

5. This was a big year (1957), but if you get one, you'll get all three: Go for the pink! Scrub the fingerprint! Ditch the gloves!

6. Even stained, they can kill. What was the murder weapon in the novella whose title suggests picking sides in the school-yard?

7. Wolfe doesn't play bridge, and he certainly never orders commercially prepared food: if he were stricken by brain fever and reversed both rules, what book would come to mind?

8. What is there about a certain arch-villain in upstate New York that suggests the sheer range of his villainy?

9. Archie twice confesses his linguistic lacunae. Where?

10. Organizationally, cooks are half again as good as eaters. Why?

11. Three hundred eighty-four units in 768 places don't tax the imagination, but the sins of the third can't be forgiven. Name the novel.

12. What weapon did Wolfe use against the French spearhead?

13. What French philosopher occasionally sounded like Fritz? Or do I have that backwards?

14. One publisher suggests Minnesota iron and another is very much a lightweight, but they did bring us NW and AG. Name them.

15. Over the course of the *Corpus,* two operatives died. Name them.

IN DECEMBER, 1997, when *The Gazette* honored The Wolfe Pack's twentieth anniversary, Henry contributed his candidates for the best twenty questions (for twenty years) that he has devised. His choices did not include the questions in the preceding quiz.

★　　★　　★

THE 20 BEST QUIZ QUESTIONS

by Henry Enberg

THE FIRST eight questions refer to book — or story — titles. What is the title of each?

1. Choice of gloves.

2. Where did the polite student say the fossil fish came from?

3. What should have been Pamela Harriman's obituary?

4. What is Tina Turner's routine?

5. Donald Trump's instruction to his architect was what?

6. What is a neutral description of NOW?

7. What was music for McLean, Burgess, and Philby?

8. Alex Trebek, Alex Trebek, Alex Trebek!

9. How do we know that "This Won't Kill You" is fiction?

10. Archie refers to a de factor copy editor in *Too Many Cooks*; where does this person work?

11. What case preceded *Fer-de-Lance*?

12. What is Mr. Wolfe's initial cash fee in *The Golden Spiders*?

13. In *Before Midnight,* the clients are described as having what brand of shirts? (The company is still around, but has been all twisted.)

14. How long is Arbor Street in *"Die Like a Dog"*?

15. How can you tell if a book Mr. Wolfe reads is a B?

16. What was the color of the Hebe's stoles?

17. What color was the carpet in the love nest in *Too Many Clients*?

18. Wolfe's tie in *"Eeny, Meeny, Murder, Mo"* could be described as what?

19. Based on the help wanted ad, Mr. Wolfe's waist was not over what?

20. What does Archie say he was to bring in *"Immune to Murder"*?

★   ★   ★

WHEN TENBY STORM assumed the role of Wolfe Pack Quiz Master ("mistress" seems pejorative), she not only devised equally challenging annual tests, she also contributed a number of variety puzzles to *The Gazette*. Here are examples of both.

MURDER VICTIMS BLACK ORCHID QUIZ
by Tenby Storm

WE'VE HAD quizzes about who dun it and how it was dun — now we have whom it was dun to! Use the clues to identify the murder victim's occupation; then name the book in which the murder occurred. [*HINT: The number of dashes are equal to the number of letters in the word or words designating the victim's occupation.* — MK]

CLUE APPEARS IN:	VICTIM'S OCCUPATION
1. Word processor	_ _ _ _ _ _ _ _
2. Writer's block	_ _ _ _ _ _ _ _
3. Hot to trot	_ _ _ _ _ _ _
4. Often found in solitary	_ _ _ _ _ _

confinement

5. Key Met player   _ _ _ _ _ _ _ _ _ _ _

6. Recipient of hand-me-downs   _ _ _ _ _ _ _

7. Provider of brilliant
   understandings   _ _ _ _ _ _ _ _ _ _ _ _ _

8. The epitome of good taste   _ _ _ _ _ _ _ _ _ _ _ _

9. Perfect in step — or in step-ins _ _ _ _ _ _ _ _ _ _

10. For whom the bells toll   _ _ _ _ _ _ _

★   ★   ★

A WOLFEAN CRYPTOGRAM

by Tenby Storm

WOULD-BE MURDERERS would do well to consider this observation, made by Nero Wolfe in *Too Many Cooks.*

SUYWDSX DL LDQMCPN YWTS YU FDCC T QTS; YWP
ADVVDHJCYDPL TNDLP DS TYYPQMYDSX YU TGUDA
YWP HUSLPEJPSHPL.

ANSWERS

BLACK ORCHID BANQUET QUIZ
— December 5, 1998

1. *Cordially Invited to Meet Death*
2. *"Before I Die," "Man Alive"*
3. *Prisoner's Base*
4. Baseball diamond
5. *"Easter Parade," "Fourth of July Picnic," "Christmas Party"*
6. Necktie in *"Eeny, Meeny, Murder, Mo"*
7. *And Four to Go*
8. A to Z — Arnold Zeck
9. *Black Mountain, Too Many Cooks*
10. Ten for Aristology but 15 masters (maitres)
11. *Gambit*
12. Beer bottle
13. Montaigne
14. Viking and Bantam
15. Johnny Keems and Orrie Cather

THE 20 BEST QUIZ QUESTIONS

1. *Black Orchids* (Black or Kid)
2. *Some Buried Caesar* (Some buried sea, sir)
3. *Death of a Doxy*
4. *Gambit* (Gams are slang for legs)
5. *Please Pass the Guilt* (gilt)
6. *Too Many Women*
7. *Trio for Blunt Instruments*

8. What is *Triple Jeopardy*

9. The Boston Red Sox win the World Series.

10. The Heinemann School of Languages (checking French)

11. The Fairmont Bank Case

12. $4.30

13. Sulka

14. Three blocks

15. Mr. Wolfe picks it up before ringing for beer; it is place-marked with a slip of paper.

16. Deep rich purple

17. Pale yellow

18. Brown silk with little yellow curlicues

19. 48 inches

20. Parsley, onions, chives, chervil, tarragon, fresh mushrooms, brandy, bread crumbs, fresh eggs, paprika, tomatoes, cheese, and Nero Wolfe.

MURDER VICTIMS BLACK ORCHID QUIZ

1. Secretary, in *If Death Ever Slept*
2. Publisher, in *"Help Wanted — Male"*
3. Horseman, in *"Bullet for One"*
4. Writer, in *The Doorbell Rang*
5. Opera Singer, in *"The Gun with Wings"*
6. Heiress, in *Prisoner's Base*
7. Shoeshine Man, in *"Kill Now — Pay Later"*
8. Restaurateur, in *The Black Mountain*
9. Chorus Girl, in *Death of a Doxy*
10. Operator, in *"The Next Witness"*

A WOLFEAN CRYPTOGRAM

Nothing is simpler than to kill a man; the difficulties arise in attempting to avoid the consequences.

Nero Wolfe — *Too Many Cooks*

Printed in the United States
55843LVS00006B/232